A FUTURE

FOR FERALS

Edited by:

Danielle Ackley-McPhail

eSpec Books

Pennsville, NJ

PUBLISHED BY
eSpec Books LLC
Danielle McPhail, Publisher
PO Box 242,
Pennsville, New Jersey 08070
www.especbooks.com

ISBN: 978-1-965266-19-9
ISBN (eBook): 978-1-965266-18-2

The docked ear cat logo is the logo of A Future For Ferals Cat Rescue

Copyediting: Greg Schauer
Cover Art and Design: Mike McPhail, McP Digital Graphics
Interior Design: Danielle McPhail

Licensed via www.shutterstock.com
Banner: Silhouette of vector black cat © artsara
Break: heart shapes within the paw pad © Md Abdus Sahid

OUR COOL CATS

Marc L. Abbott	Lisa Kruse
Danielle Ackley-McPhail	Mike McPhail
Rigel Ailur	Bernie Mojzes
Grace Bridges	Nancy Jane Moore
Christopher J. Burke	Aaron Rosenberg
Amber Davis	Lawrence M. Schoen
Keith R.A. DeCandido	Jean Marie Ward
Carol Gyzander	Jeff Young

Global Cat Day and National Feral Cat Day

October 16
https://globalcatday.org/about/

While there are many, many rescues across the country and around the world, here are a few we've come across that we wanted to share.

Alley Cat Allies

https://www.alleycat.org/ -

Humane Rescue Alliance

https://www.humanerescuealliance.org/

Clawd found his forever home, but not all kitties are so lucky

FOR OUR ANGEL CATS
ALWAYS IN OUR HEARTS

Bandit (Mau)	Ralph	Pepper
Tiger	Marguerite	Ariel
Bootsie	Chauvelin	Mimi
Hootch	Percy	Frankie Blue-Eyes
Mandy	Marie	Ash
Kat	Duchess	Burton
Baby	Nikki	Archie
Alley	Rigel	Arwen
Goodyear	King of the Jungle	Brandee
Rex	Lister	Buzzee
Kismet	Joby	The Rev
Cuddle Bug	Nelly	Nicky
Merry	Tal	Patia
Curio	Bast	Kodi
Magnus	Bonnie	Max!
Tuppence	Clyde	Hex
Echo	Duzell	Socks
Munchkin	Molly	Mozart
Mithril	Rascal	Scrabble
Audrey Kitty	Trooper	Belle
Benjamin	'Neaker	Sprite
Daisy	Miss Audrey	Trooper
Nevar	Benjamin Franklin Cat	Quill
Bleys	Hobbs	Peppercorn Underfoot
Mahasamatman	Boodles	

AND FOR OUR "COLONY KITTIES"
YOUR PERSON LOVES YOU EXTRA-SPECIAL

Spot (Sweetie)	Eve	Squeaks
Spec	Midnight	Jean
Karma	Gizmo	Storm
Shiloh	Tigger	Roguee
Pandora	Logan	Boris

eSpec's spokescat, Merry, encourages you to read.

PLEASE, PLEASE READ...

I'M NOT USUALLY BIG ON INTRODUCTIONS; HECK, A LOT OF PEOPLE DON'T really read them anyway, but here it goes. In all of my years of compiling anthologies it has always been about a cool, fun idea. A concept hits me, a catchy title follows along and I am off and running!

This one isn't any different in that regard, except it is.

A Future for Ferals has a heart, and a cause. (And a sequel!) The title itself is taken from the name of a cat rescue run by a former coworker. In our time together on the clock it was difficult not to get caught up in the real-life drama that is cat rescue. I heard all of the stories, from late-night trapping sessions to being called in to clear out a cat hoarder's house to whatever other adventure came next.

Rescue is not an easy calling, whether it is cats or some other species. It is hard work with usually no pay, often not enough volunteers, and very little thanks beyond (hopefully) the satisfaction of making life better for another living creature. When donations are low, rescuers draw on their own funds to take care of their temporary charges, and not even just the basics of food, shelter, and necessities, but medical costs or even end-of-life care.

This collection seeks to share some of that burden. The profits from the campaign that funded these books have already been sent to A Future for Ferals, a 501c3 registered charity, to mitigate the costs of rescuing over fifty cats in one day from a hoarder house. Of the fifty cats, only two had been neutered. The vet bill was over $4000 to neuter the rest and take care of the necessary medical care some of the cats needed resulting from neglect.

This is one group of many around the world seeking to make life better for abandoned and feral cats (and other animals) and the communities where they live. We and our authors would like to support them in their efforts.

All of the stories you will read here have been donated. All profits from future sales will be donated to various cat rescues for the lifetime of this anthology.

Given the nature of the book, some of these stories are reprints, others are newly written. And for once, the genres are mixed, so my apologies in advance if not all of the stories are to your taste or the collection feels uneven. In the interest of not getting monotonous, they aren't necessarily all about cat rescue, though all are about cats. What we have also done, however, is include personal accounts between the stories, as well as short informational pieces about various aspects that go into cat rescue. Why? Because cat overpopulation is rapidly increasing and any effort we can make to educate and improve that situation helps.

We hope you will enjoy everything we have brought together, and share word of this collection with others. Perhaps even gift a copy to someone you know has a heart for the kitties as well.

Thank you for reading…

Danielle Ackley-McPhail
Editor and Publisher

Our Angel Cat, Magnus, on his Gotcha Day.

With multiple health issues, he wasn't with us long, just a few years, but we still feel his love. He weighed just five pounds in this picture and suffered from untreated hyperthyroidism.

A FUTURE FOR FERALS
CAT RESCUE

A Future for Ferals cat rescue is a 501c3 non-profit foster-based organization that was started in 2021 to specifically help the cats that are typically overlooked in a normal shelter setting when it comes to adoptions such as older cats, disabled cats, those with behavior issues, and more. We got started after our founder worked in a county shelter and saw the total disregard and lack of care when it came to these types of cats there and knew something better could be done for them.

A feral cat is an unsocialized cat that does not want to interact and will typically avoid humans, with that being said "a future for ferals" means to us less euthanasia of feral cats especially in the county shelters, more socializing when and if possible, more barn homes when absolutely needed, more trap, neuter, and return (TNR) and definitely more public education and compassion for the topic.

Other than adoptions, our other heavily focused goal is TNR and spay/neuter in general to help reduce the cat population. The world is currently in a cat overpopulation crisis with there being more cats than homes for them available. We will never adopt our way out of the population crisis without TNR/spay and neuter of all cats. Since starting the rescue in 2021 we have been able to help TNR hundreds of cats each year and that does not even include our adoptable cats being spayed/neutered, or our outreach program that we offer to assist our local communities with low cost spay/neuter appointments. We believe every cat should be spayed/neutered as both genders becoming territorial and acting out if hormones are not in check. Avoiding these things happening will in turn help with less surrenders and less abandonment, which is why we offer an outreach program for low-cost appointments.

We are completely foster-based, meaning we have volunteers who open up their homes to our cats and take care of them until they are adopted into their forever homes. We do not have a physical location with an adoption center like a typical shelter. This unfortunately does limit us with intakes though, as we can only intake if we have a foster home lined up for that cat. We often have over one hundred cats in foster care awaiting their forever homes, with many being long-term residents due to the types of cats we focus on, but since starting in 2021 we have successfully adopted out over five hundred cats into loving homes. We would never have been able to do this without having such wonderful fosterers offering assistance.

Angelina Commisso

Harriet - a Future for Ferals former rescue

CONTENTS

Curio cat, where you at? Getting into Trouble!

COLONY CARGO
Carol Gyzander

DAY 1

Ship's Instructions to crew: Launch successful. Extended voyage progresses on track. Perform inspection round twice daily and press All Clear when complete.

Personal Log: I am Cohrn, and this is my first entry here. I hope I am doing it right. We have just blasted off from the human space station as a last-minute replacement crew on this cargo ship. My lovely wife, Bagg, and I are on our way to the Interstellar Writer Colony, where we will join our fellow Zagrosian writers-in-exile and writers from other worlds. Zoot be praised!

"Oh, Bagg, do you think this will be a good trip?" Cohrn stared at the ship's system console in their new living quarters as he finished his log entry, the screen reflecting his blue reptilian skin. "I mean, seriously, darling, I'm worried that being on this human ship for three years will make us like them. They seem to be so… I don't know, stupid?"

Bagg's forked tongue flicked out of her mouth. "Cohrn, how can you say that? They gave us this job. It will get us to the writer colony where we belong!"

Cohrn rubbed the frill on the top of his head with one claw. "Yes, they said it was required to have a sentient presence on board, even though the ship functions automatically. But face it, we have no experience operating a spaceship, especially a human one. I think the humans assume we know what we're doing just because they regard us as aliens. It's rather species-ist, don't you think?"

His Zagrosian mate bustled around the small cabin in the quarters where they would be living for the three-year voyage. She pulled items out of their travel cases, looking around for a place to put them.

"I don't really care, dear. As long as we got out of human space quickly, so that I didn't have to look at their eyes any longer. Those round irises totally creeped me out, and a two-day layover was more than enough. Hey, look. Here are all your writing talismans."

She passed him a small metal container. "Do you want to set them up by the console where you'll be writing?"

"Yesss, I've been wondering where those were! My muses." Cohrn opened the container and reverently extracted a series of small, large-headed reptilian figures. Placing them in a row in front of the system console and his story cube, he touched each one on the top and smiled as the heads bobbled about. "Now, *this* feels more like home. Is there anything I can do to help you?"

Bagg stood in the middle of the room, looking around, her clawed hand covering her mouth. "Where are we supposed to sleep?"

His gaze fell upon a rectangular pad atop a low platform. "This looks pretty comfy, and it has soft, movable fibers on top. Do you think this is what the humans use for a nest?"

She tapped her claws upon her chin. "Sssss. Why is it up in the air? A nest should be at ground level."

Cohrn dragged the pad onto the floor. Then, ruffling up the covers on the top, he stood back and looked at the results with his head tilted to one side. "How's that? I can move the frame out of the way into the cargo bay later."

Bagg crawled onto the soft mound and nestled in. "Yesss. I think this will do." She stroked the surface and looked at Cohrn from under her second eye membranes. Her long tongue flicked out between her sharp teeth. "Do you want to try it out?"

Cohrn's tail lashed from side to side. "Yesss, you little seductress, but the message on the screen tells me I should walk up and down the corridors to check everything and then push the button. Zoot knows what I'm looking for, but I'd better do what the system tells me. I will be back. But…" He held his clawed hands up between them. "You know we can't start a brood while on the ship."

Bagg hissed softly and ducked her head. "I will keep unpacking."

DAY 2

Personal Log: Well, everything seems to be quiet. I walked around to check the ship like I'm supposed to, and it was good exercise. I don't see anything I need to do for maintenance, and the ship hasn't given me any instructions, so I guess we have some writing time. Ha! Who am I kidding? We actually have three whole years to ourselves — I'm going to get a lot more writing done. And reading. Really enjoying the peace and quiet.

DAY 3

Personal Log: I heard strange noises down the empty corridors. It's like a peculiar moaning. When I went there, I didn't see anything, but since we've been on board, I sometimes catch a glimpse of movement out of the corner of my eye. The moaning noise wakes me at night, and I must put my pillow over my head — such a sad and lonely sound.

DAY 4

Ship's Instructions to crew: WARNING! Living quarters temperature below acceptable range. Blockage detected in ventilation system — maintenance required.

Personal Log: After crawling around in the ventilation ducts and cleaning them out, I realized just how creepy it is to be alone out here. Every move I made reverberated around in those metal tubes, and I kept thinking something was behind me. I'm sure it's nothing — just an echo — but I want to see Bagg and show her what I found.

"Lovey, did you get everything fixed? It's awfully cold in here, and I can't think straight. I don't know how those humans can stand it." Bagg stood with her arms wrapped around herself as Cohrn entered the living quarters. "What on earth is that?"

Cohrn held out the mess of soft fluff in his hand. "This is what I found in the ventilation ducts, blocking the airflow. It should get warmer now that I've cleared it, but I have no idea how it got there. And the ventilation grate was open a little bit, too, so I closed it up tight."

"Huh." Bagg's delicate blue features crinkled as she came to examine the fluff. "And now it's all over you, too. That looks like what humans have on top of their heads. What would it be doing in the ventilation system?"

"No clue, but maybe humans aren't the only animals with that stuff on them. If I knew how to do more on their computer, I could look it up, but I'm a little afraid to start pushing other buttons. And you know what the other creepy thing was?"

"What? There's *more*?"

Cohrn reached his clawed hand into the sack he carried across one shoulder and pulled out a fistful of tiny bones — pointy skulls with little teeth, teeny-tiny finger bones ending in sharp claws, and little-bitty tails. "They're tiny, but there were lots of them."

"Are those… reptilian, like us? Cohrn, are we in danger?" She clutched his forearm. "Is there something in here that feeds on reptiles?"

"No, I don't think so. I read about these in the maintenance manual, once I found a version in Zagrosian, which says they are common and can be a real problem." At her blank look, he continued, "I think they're a pest called 'mice' that are known to infest some ships, eating away at some of the wires and making problems. But here they are, apparently, just tiny prey eaten by… whatever left the fluff."

DAY 10

Personal Log: There's no further blockage in the ventilation system, and the access panel remains closed. But when I was on my rounds, I kept feeling yet again like I was seeing something out of the corner of my eye. When I turned around, there was nothing there. Spooky.

Bagg has holed up in our quarters and refuses to walk the ship's corridors with me. Instead, she spends all her time trilling her tale into the story cube or cleaning the room. I fear this is one of the first stages of nesting — she assures me there will be no eggs, no brood of hatchlings while we are on the ship. But I can tell she longs for them.

I miss her company.

DAY 11

Ship's Instructions to crew: WARNING! Breach detected in cargo container. Commence investigation.

Personal Log: Okay, this is seriously creepy. Bagg finally made me move that frame down to the cargo hold last week. Now there's damage to a cargo pod that didn't appear on the surveillance system until after I went in there—something must have followed me in! What the freak is this ship carrying to the writer colony?

I sealed the cargo pod to prevent further access and swept up all the pellet-sized stuff strewn across the floor. Crunchy underfoot, but it smells somewhat like fishy. Took it back to the galley and will analyze it to see if it is edible, as we are already tremendously sick of human food.

"Bagg, you won't believe what I found in the cargo bay." Cohrn dropped the sack of pellets in the cabin. "I'm not sure what it is, but it smells like fishy from home!"

Bagg lifted her head and paused her writing for a moment. "Fishy? Oh, I love fishy. Is this really something we can eat?"

"I don't know, but if I can figure out how to get the computer to analyze it, we'll have more information. I will stow it in the galley, as I don't want to go back in the cargo pod now that I've sealed the hole."

"Hole? What made a hole?" Bagg's eyes went big and round, and she wrapped her arms around herself.

Cohrn rushed over and stroked her frill. "No worries, lovey. Just some maintenance I had to do."

Bagg nodded and turned back to her story cube.

DAY 12

Personal Log: Glad to say the heat is still working fine, but now I'm a little weirded out that some of our food is disappearing from the galley. Nothing major, but I left pieces of something the humans call "cheese" out on the table after lunch, and when I came back after my rounds, it was gone. It was like the plate was licked clean. Did I really leave it out? Or am I getting a little space happy? They told me this could be a problem on these long routes.

DAY 13

Personal Log: Okay, yeah, I know the computer says there are no further problems with the ventilation, but it looks to me like there are marks on that hatch where it had been opened before. Like *claw* marks. And that cargo pod was ripped open again, with more pellet stuff strewn around. Sealed it up—again.

What the freak.

DAY 14

Personal Log: I'm seeing things. I'm pretty sure I'm seeing things. *Am* I seeing things? Movement appears under the edge of a storage pod or flashes around a corner when I get near, but nothing triggers the system sensors. What the freak?

DAY 15

Personal Log: There's nothing to report—at least, not anything I can write down in the official record.

First, I thought having the fluff—and those bones—in the ventilation system was creepy. Now I've found a pile of what seems to be poop in the corner of the galley storage room. *Poop.* And more food has been disappearing, I think. I cleaned up the poop and put it in cryostorage, labeled Unknown Specimen Two.

Not telling Bagg about it. She barely talks to me anyway these days—always trilling at her story cube until all hours. It seems my spouse is disappearing into the story world she's writing about a family on our home planet—and I have writer's block. Go figure.

DAY 16

Personal Log: I put out some food last night just to see if I imagined it. All the "vegetable" units were still there in the morning, but the "tuna" units were gone. And more poop. But— no yowling. That's something, right? At least I got some sleep.

DAY 17

Personal Log: Oh, my gods. I had to know, so I sat in the galley perusing a story cube last night to keep watch. I waited and tried not to move. After a long while, I saw a shape out of the corner of my eye, approaching cautiously like a shadow. It hugged the wall and slunk along near the cabinet, heading for the table where I had left the food. I made the mistake of moving, though, and it dashed away—all I saw was a flash of teeth, claws, and pointy ears. Scary! What is this thing?

DAY 18

Personal Log: I left no food out, and the pellet container I had stowed in the galley was tipped over again this morning and spilled all over the floor. We had found it unpalatable, but do the pellets attract the… whatever-it-is?

DAY 19

Personal Log: I haven't seen the fluff-creature for two days since I scared it—or should I say since it scared me. But the food I've left out is gone every morning, and there's poop left in the same corner every day. So I clean it but no longer bother saving it in cryostorage.

Had no idea I would be a janitor on this voyage. Or a zookeeper.

DAY 23

Personal Log: The fluff-creature and I have come to an understanding. I leave the food out, and it does not spill the pellets and make a mess. I've seen it loitering under the cabinet, and the reflection of eyes peer back at me—round eyes with vertical irises like mine. At least that's familiar. When I sit very still, I sometimes feel warm pressure along my leg, but it runs and disappears when I turn toward it—all I see is a fluffy orange tail disappearing under the cabinets.

And orange fluff all over my leg.

DAY 24

Personal Log: I touched it today! Put my claws down and stroked the top of it as it rubbed on my leg. Soft, warm, felt clean. When I tried to lean over to reach it more, it turned and made a weird noise—like hot air coming out of a hole in the ventilation system. Then it swiped at me, and oh, those claws—like razors! I'm only bleeding a little bit.

DAY 25

Personal Log: I nearly freaked out this morning. Sat at the table eating, and the fluff-creature jumped right up on the table. Stared me down as it ate part of my breakfast. I did not object because, hey, I didn't want to get clawed again. Delicate eater — but oh, those fangs. I didn't dare move.

DAY 29

Personal Log: Fluff-creature has been eating my breakfast every day. It forces me to sit still and watch it — that hissing noise when I move is really intimidating. Because yeah, I remember those bones I found in the ventilation system. I'm not stupid.

DAY 31

Personal Log: It's started attacking me as I eat. Nothing physically damaging anymore, but it holds me in thrall with those big eyes and shows me its dominance by wiping its face on me after it consumes my food. Creepy — it walks back and forth on the table and makes a low rumbling sound as it wipes on me. I'm afraid to move.

DAY 35

Personal Log: I'm getting a little worried about supplies if it continues to eat our food. Worried we'll run out. So, a few days ago, I put a plate of those fishy pellets on the table when I ate my breakfast. It seems to like the stuff and sits there waiting for me to place the dish every morning.

DAY 41

Personal Log: Now I'm on a schedule, and it's not mine! The fluff-creature screams at me if I'm late getting its breakfast. Such a dreadful noise — ear-piercing and intense. No letup until I serve the pellets. It appears whenever I sit at the table or at the system console to make my log entries or at my story cube — it walks back and forth so I cannot see the screen and sheds fluff all over the keyboard. Always forcing me to be submissive while using me as a cleaning post.

DAY 51

Personal Log: Okay, this was new. It walked directly on me. I was sitting in the comfy chair, and it jumped up on me and walked back and forth, probably to show its dominance. Then it squatted down on my lap and forced me to stay still. I was expecting it to poop, but it just curled up and made that scary rumbly sound. There was nothing to do while I sat there, so I finally trilled some words into my story cube for the first time in weeks. After a while, it left.

My lap felt cold where it had been.

DAY 54

Personal Log: There are two of them! Both came out to eat while I was there; the new one is black and white. I dared not move for fear of provoking this second one's claws — it is much larger around the middle than the first. Its belly almost touches the floor. Clearly very strong.

DAY 56

Personal Log: Today, the orange one was by itself. It settled on my lap again and made that little rumbling noise as it forced me to sit in the chair and trill my words. I took a risk and stroked its pelt.

It was soft and warm.

DAY 72

Personal Log: I'm getting more writing work done these days. The orange fluff-creature sits on my lap daily while I'm at the story cube. Most of the time, I can keep it off the keys. I think it makes me feel less lonely. But I haven't seen the black-and-white one in a week. Where could it be? I hope… I hope it's okay.

DAY 74

Personal Log: Oh, sweet mother of the stars! There are more of them! The black-and-white one has reappeared with seven tiny ones — some orange, some black and white, and some striped. It must have been hatching its eggs.

The little ones are adorable. I never thought I'd say that about a creature that infests the ship and holds me in thrall to do its bidding. But yeah.

DAY 78

Personal Log: Bagg has fallen in love with the little ones! She strokes them, cuddles them, and takes them into our nest to sleep, so I have little room. But I am delighted to see her returning to me from her story world. And, of course, we can't have our own hatchlings yet, so I would do anything to keep her happy!

I've made multiple trips to the cargo bay for more pellets. After checking the marking on the first pod that was opened, I discovered that the humans call them some strange six-letter word where the middle consonants repeat. While this should theoretically make it easier to locate the correct pods, I am still having trouble reading all the human words to find them.

DAY 365

Personal Log: Our voyage is now one-third complete. The fluff-creatures have continued to reproduce at an alarming rate. I estimate there are now hundreds of them. I want to feed them less and slow them down, but Bagg's having none of it—even though she suggests they are reproducing so fast because of the plentiful food supply.

Heading for the cargo bay with a transport sled and a crowbar. Going to have to break open all the cargo pods until I can find more of the right ones marked with six letters.

We're going to be in trouble over the damaged cargo and the infestation of the ship when we get to the writer colony. I sure hope the writers there like these fluff-creatures. Who knew we'd get into such trouble with "KIBBLE"?

Echo

Munchkin

THE CAT AND THE DRAGON
Grace Bridges

As if the summer day wasn't warm enough already, steam rose lazily from the drains and gutters of Rotorua. Somewhere far below, a hot spring's emergence had broken through the man-made pipes again and now found its way up, up to the world of light, te ao marama.

A lanky yellow street cat dodged a plume of steam where it split into hazy stripes over a metal grille, then she loped on through the back alleys and parks. For her, safety lay away from the busy central city. Instinct and hunger called her to watch the seagulls at the shoreline; perhaps one would be slow enough for her to catch today.

Besides, she remembered—with some yearning—a person who often sat on the boardwalk at lake's edge, surveying the cloudy water in the lake. A person of indeterminate appearance but reasonably advanced age; a person who had smiled at her and shared bits of a picnic on occasion.

The cat made her way down one final block toward the shore, passing a couple of hotels. She dodged the door of the last one as a crowd of oddly-dressed humans tumbled out, laughing; some wore jingly metallic accessories, others strange headgear, while some carried gnarled sticks and one even looked like he had pointed ears. The cat cocked one of her own ears at this; humans were not supposed to look like that!

She skirted the crowd and trotted off toward the boardwalk, tail held high. Was her friend here? She sniffed the air, laden with the aromas of warm sulfur and seagull guano. The birds wheeled above, eyeing her closely but keeping their distance.

Yes—that hint of a scent—it was her person. She approached the wooden bench from behind and curled around the stubby legs before it. The person greeted her with soft and friendly tones, but spread empty hands, looking along the shore to the south. *Yes, yes,* said the cat's stomach. *That's where the great yellow house of food is.* She was pleased when the person creaked upright, patted her goodbye, and set off in that direction; perhaps there would be food in a little while, if she just waited.

Well, waited nearby, at least. The cat pushed through the gap in the boardwalk's railings and paced out over the sulfur rock. Gulls shrieked when she got too near a nest, so she detoured toward the waterline, but kept watch anyway, seating her thin hips on the thermally warmed stone.

The sun burst out from behind a cloud, and the cat half-closed her eyes for a moment, basking in the heat from above and below. Before she could stretch and relax her muscles, something huffed nearby, and she became fully alert in an instant. Her head turned toward the odd disturbance.

Fire. She did not know its name, but she knew what it was. A small clump of powdery sulfur burned all by itself not two feet from her nose. Hair rose along her back and her tail puffed up.

She backed away, afraid; her back paw sploshed into the edge of the lake water.

Fire or not, she marched back up the rocks, shaking her paw, then sat down to give it a good lick. And that's when it happened.

Who left a great ruddy lake just exactly there, anyway? How inconvenient of them.

The cat blinked. *What's all this then — I'm stringing words together in my head. I know what they mean. I think, therefore…*

She remembered just a few moments ago, when she had lived on instinct alone, nothing more. Of course it was adequate, it was how all cats existed. But now that she was discovering the power of actual thought, her prior awareness seemed much inferior.

Lick, lick. The foot was mostly dry. She set it down and eyed the glowing sulfur with rather more consideration than before. The flame was only just visible, a blueness engulfing the stone that now melted into a puddle of viscous red. *Sulfur deposits are liable to spontaneously combust if the sunshine is strong enough.* She flicked an ear, shook her head. *How do I know these things?*

She turned her head, and her gaze fell on the row of hotels, suddenly understanding that the pointy-eared human was just dressing up for fun, the same as the others with him. *Fake ears. I know about cosplay, a lot of it goes on here after all. I just never had a name for it before.*

She shook herself, but the strange feeling did not dissipate. Her eyes panned and took in the view of the bay, the noisy gulls with their animal instincts, the milky water where the thermal springs lurked below. The panorama was familiar, but now she regarded it with a sharpness that was clearly unrelated to her magnificent feline vision.

Oh. That's new, too. Well, she had always had her rightful share of catitude, the non-verbal kind. This *wordy* attitude was a whole other level. Her eyelids drooped in a smile. She could get used to this.

The sulfur fire flared up, blue-white and transparent, and she thought it must be going out. Such a little pebble to burn so long alone! But as she watched, the shape of the flame extended and spread, gaining clear edges and a shape that remained stable even as it flickered.

That's not normal. Neither was thinking in words, but fires certainly weren't supposed to behave like that, even weird mineral fires on thermally heated shores.

The shape morphed into something resembling a cat's head. Suddenly the street moggy had thoughts of Bast or perhaps some other feline deity — how *could* she know these things? — an entity from the unseen world grew solid before her, though made of delicate fire.

All of her thoughts were impossible, including *having* thoughts in the first place. But she kept her perfect poise, observing the creature before her and no doubt likewise being observed.

Not a cat. A dragon. The difference was delicate, and she looked away. Not Bast, then.

The body made of flames rose farther out of the ground until finally it stood before her, four sinewed legs, a pair of strong wings, a fierce kind of face she thought couldn't be entirely non-feline in nature. The sulfur pebble burned on, a small flicker against the horse-sized being who now paced a small circle around the immediate area.

The cawing of gulls had stopped entirely, and a glance told the cat they had all vanished away. Had they seen what was happening? Could they? People walking by on the boardwalk not twenty feet away paid no attention, leading her to believe they were unable to perceive the dragon.

A sound brought her attention back to the dragon. A rustling, burning sort of voice, and to her surprise, she understood it.

"Kua karanga koe i ahau."

The cat comprehended at once that the creature spoke Māori, and also that she could understand it without translating. *A language of the heart. Wait, so that means my head speaks a different language…* Her brain lit up more with every moment. It would hurt if it wasn't so beautiful.

The dragon went on smoothly in Māori. "You called me here, to the burning stone. Why?"

Sunshine called you here, then. The stone burns of its own self in the sun.

The dragon frowned down at her. Had it heard her thoughts? Apparently so, for it replied. "You are sunshine, then."

Am I? She glanced down at her golden self and spared a self-conscious lick to her shoulder. *I'm certainly the right shade of yellow.*

The dragon blinked slowly, a friendly gesture. "Hello, Sunshine. Why did you call me?"

I don't think I did. You know, around here sometimes things burn without help.

"I do have a certain… connection to the sun, myself. But I am here now."

What are you going to do? Sunshine watched as the creature stopped its pacing and looked at her.

"I do not know. No human has called me. You have no request yourself."

Is this a problem for you?

"Only because it should not happen. I come when the humans call in the right way. The proper call has been made… without humans."

Sunshine sauntered over to the burning sulfur pebble. Beside it, a patch of yellow gleamed among the other, dimmer rocks. *That'll be why. Some seagull has scratched the top off this sulfur deposit, so the sunshine can set it alight. It's exposed.*

"Kei te manea koe, e ngeru," said the dragon. Sunshine restrained a snort. Of course she was clever. *No need to state the obvious, friend taniwha.*

Taniwha, of course. More brand-new puzzle pieces fell into place behind Sunshine's sharp eyes. *Rotorua is famous for its taniwha. I am pleased to meet you.*

The dragon chuckled softly, a deep rumbling crackle of fire. "In any case, you are right. These birds have exposed the sulfur to the heat of the sun, and that means I can be called… by accident."

Something's wrong with this picture.

The taniwha nodded its enormous head. "Can you help me?"

Me? Help you? Surely, Mr. Taniwha, you are the stronger of us two.

"Kaore he tāne."

Not a mister. Okay, fine. Miss? Mrs.?

"Not that either. It doesn't matter. Back to the point. Will you help?"

Depends what it is you want done. I'm just a cat, even though I'm so fabulous.

"Ko te mea nui… The important thing is, I am not a physical form. I can take on a physical shape with great effort, but this is not an emergency."

Sunshine thought she could tell where he — she? — was going with this. *You want me to do something physical for you.*

"Ae, little Sunshine. You said the birds uncovered that patch of sulfur. Do you think you could cover it again?"

Things became clear. Sunshine pointed her nose in the air. *You want me to DIG?*

"I cannot do it. But if it is not done, that patch or others like it will burn up in the sun, and I will be called from my rest without reason again."

With this, Sunshine experienced deep empathy. She didn't like being woken up for nothing either. *If I cover this patch, what will you do for me?*

"You don't know what I have done for you already? Think about it."

Sunshine did so, and the answer was clear as day. *It's you! This is your power that — somehow turned my brain on.* She bared her long front teeth ever so slightly. *Will this… thinking… remain after you return to your bed?*

"I will see if I can make it so. I need you to make sure none of this sulfur burns needlessly."

Makes sense. Sunshine even nodded, just as she'd seen humans do often. Now she knew what it meant. *If my thinking sleeps as before, I will not know to keep the sulfur buried.*

"True enough. Let me touch your mind, to keep it sharp if I can."

Sunshine flattened her ears against her head. *I don't like it. But I suppose you must.* This day had been an enormous pile of impossible things so far. One more made little difference at this point.

The dragon nodded and reached out a fiery wingtip. It brushed the top of Sunshine's head, and she shivered despite the blaze of heat.

"Ngā mihi," said the taniwha. Thank you.

You're welcome, I'm sure. Thank you for a most enlightening day. I do have one other request…

"Nō reira, kōrero mai." Therefore, speak it to me.

Tell my person my new name. Sunshine glanced over her shoulder at the hunched figure even now hurrying back from the shop in the next block over.

The taniwha followed her gaze and laughed. "Your person has a name, too, you know. That's Harley, who has also received gifts from my kind."

How do you know Harley's name?

Another laugh. "Harley is my person, too."

Sunshine clambered over the boulders to the patch of sulfur, where she scratched at inert sandstones and loose pumice until only a glimmer of yellow remained. Easy enough. Before she swiped a paw over the last of it, she looked up at the dragon again and saw that the original pebble was about to go out. She and the dragon exchanged another slow blink, and she turned back to her task. A swipe, a kick, and it was done — thankfully there were no other bits of naked sulfur in sight. *But who knows what the birds will get up to, I'll have to keep an eye out —*

"I'm sorry. It's not working," said the taniwha, fading right alongside the last of the sulfur flame and Sunshine's clarity of thought. "I may yet call on you to awaken again…"

The cat found herself alone on the lakeshore, contemplating her very dusty paws. She set about cleaning them.

Harley rushed back from the supermarket, clutching a packet of cat treats and a little slice of fresh fish. But the boardwalk was empty. *Just my luck, that cat's gone and vanished again even though I asked it to stay.*

Sigh. Harley leaned on the railing and surveyed the expanse of sulfur-filled rock where the gulls nested. Such a familiar sight; the sight of home, really. *Wait, what's that?* Harley's eyes narrowed. Sure enough, way out there on the rocks, the golden cat licked at her paws like she hadn't a care in the world.

"Oi!" said Harley. *Blimmin' cat needs a name. I see her around often enough.*

The cat looked up, and Harley thought there was a trace of feline smile around her eyes, but she kept right on licking that paw. "Don't make me come over there."

Harley waited a bare minute. The cat remained planted where she was. "Fine. I'm coming." Around the end of the railing, across the pale rough stone and some larger rocky outcrops. Harley peered at the ground, suspicious. Was that the scent of burning?

Finally, Harley approached the cat. "You'll be wanting some of this, little missy."

The cat smelled fish at last and approached, sniffing at the package while Harley tore it open.

Some moments later, Harley's eye fell upon a disturbed patch of ground. A burnt-out pebble rested beside a series of burn marks… that strongly resembled… *letters?*

Harley stepped closer to examine the markings, sounding out the word hidden in plain sight. "Tama-nui-te-rā." A long, low whistle caught the cat's attention, but she returned immediately to her fish. Harley stared at the ground a little longer, then at the sky, and the cat. "The name of the sun himself, eh? I guess he set the sulfur on fire again. Hope there's no more while I'm standing here."

The cat finished the fish and came seeking the other treats, her purr a sudden loud rumble. Harley opened the bag and spilled some out, and the cat allowed herself to be patted as she ate.

"Little golden missy," said Harley. "I think your name will have to be Sunshine."

"The Cat and the Dragon" by Grace Bridges, first published as "Sulphur and Sunshine" in Something Strange Happened in Rotorua, *published by GeyserCon / Speculative Fiction New Zealand, 2019.*

CAT COLONIES
Lisa Kruse

AT 1:22 PM A POLICEMAN BANGED ON THE DOOR OF MY FRIEND CATHY'S house. The neighbor had complained again about all the stray cats on the property. Cathy had been told the last time that she had to stop feeding and taking care of them or she would be fined. But she had a surprise for him this time. As the officer began speaking Cathy held up her hand. When she had his attention she pointed to the certificate taped on the window and stepped back to let him read it.

Because, you see, our county had a new law. If you had a "feral cat colony" that you fed and took care of, you could now register the colony, and it would be protected from the police or animal control touching your cats. On your side, you agree to take full ownership of these cats and provide for the humane management of an outdoor colony. You agree to feed them, get their shots, spay or neuter them, and get them chipped to your address so they could be returned if they wandered off. Our local PAWS shelter was sponsoring these colonies too! You could apply to be a registered colony, and PAWS would absorb the cost of medical for those specific cats for as long as they had medical services on the property. Cats had to have names and a specific place to sleep.

For my colony, we have large, insulated bins with self-warming beds placed around the bushes outside and a cat door on the door to our heated porch with more beds, a couch and warm blankets, hard food, and water feeders too. It is very cold here in the winter, sometimes with too much snow for the cats to go anywhere so they are given a nice warm place of their own to stay.

I only wish I could have seen the look on the neighbor's face when the policeman told them there was nothing they could do about Cathy's cats as it was now a legally protected colony.

We had been feeding any strays that came to our property, but we were worried about them, especially when one neighbor bragged about putting out pans of chopped hot dogs soaking in antifreeze to kill them. Once we were a legal, registered colony the police had to investigate when we made a complaint about a situation that was hurting our cats. Now I look at "our" cats. They are every bit our cats as the ones we adopted ourselves. We have two house cats that were left behind when an older gentleman moved and tossed them out. Both unspayed females that were almost immediately pregnant. We also have the cat from the house next door that was left locked inside the house when the family moved away, and we have the pure ferals that come every day for food but don't want to be touched or sleep in a bed, but will stay in the outside shelters when it's cold. All of these are protected under the Colony law once we trap, neuter, and chip them. We enclosed the empty lot that we own in a high fence to encourage the cats to stay on the property and make them feel safe, and most of them do. This Legal Colony law has been transformative for so many colonies. We still worry about the cats that come and go but we don't have to worry as much anymore about the ones that have chosen to make our yard and porch their homes.

Kruse Colony Ferals

MOST DEAD BODIES IN A CONFINED SPACE

Jean Marie Ward

"Just think, Muldoon — our very first X-file!"

I covered my ears, but I knew it wouldn't help. Sally's a cute bit of fluff, but once she starts talking in exclamation points there's no turning back. You're going to do what she wants you to do sooner or later. So, you might as well take it and like it. I turned to the death trap at the back of the cavernous garage.

The corroded tin box looked like a mad scientist's version of one of those kiddie rides people rent for picnics. To operate this one, you wound a large crank, then convinced your marks that they'd win a prize if they could crawl through the open-ended cylinder in the center of the box in thirty seconds or less. But once the patsies had clambered into the drum, their weight tripped a spring that flipped them into the front of the box. Depending on whether the front door was closed or open, they either wound up "in jail," or they tumbled out on the ground giggling and disoriented.

That's the way it was supposed to work, but here something went terribly wrong. The first body sprawled almost upright in the open front bay as if flattened against the far wall by a giant fist. Her left arm reached skyward. Her lips curled back from gums dried to the color of blood, frozen in a scream of ontological despair against the meaninglessness of existence and the consequent certainty of oblivion.

At least that's how Fox Mulder would've put it.

I wondered why nobody had heard her cry for help. More to the point, why hadn't anybody smelled her and the other withered and deflated bodies wedged into the open drum?

One head sagged out of the opening on the left side of the drum, the soles of one set of feet indicated a body facing the other direction. I started counting before I realized what I was doing. I stopped at four, coughing back the sour taste that rose up my throat. I told myself the tarry scent of oil-stained concrete mixed with mouse droppings and dust from the ragged sacks of birdseed stacked near the trap disagreed with my lunch. Except I hadn't eaten lunch.

"Alien harvesting?" Sally chirped hopefully as she tried to dodge around me to get a better view. Did I mention she identified with a certain red-haired TV character whose name also begins with "S"?

"Cheese Louise," Jerry groaned, hunching his shoulders and ducking his head as if he could make like a turtle and disappear for a while. "I should've never brought you guys into it. I just thought you oughta know what was happening."

"Yeah, a real humanitarian," I said. Someone hidden in the shadows giggled. "What are you and your cousin doing around here anyway? The Boss already booted you off the property once. You know what'll happen if she catches you back here. It would go a lot better for you if you just got lost and left this to the guys in uniform."

Sally tried to pout. "Thomas Aloysius Muldoon, you're no fun at all. If we leave it to the uniforms, we'll never know what happened. We could be in danger, too, you know."

"When was the last time you were in the garage, Sally? Hey! Get back!" I blocked her move toward the trap just in time.

"But somebody needs to examine the bodies," she protested.

"Leave it to the experts. The last I heard, watching medical shows does not qualify you for an M.D. But all those cop shows you watch should've taught you not to contaminate the scene of a crime. People think you've got something to do with it, and the real killer gets away."

Sally narrowed her eyes and tilted her head this way and that as if considering a particularly difficult problem: me. Moving in for the kill, she tangled herself in my arms and rubbed her temple against my cheek. "Muldoon," she purred, her breath ruffling my hair, "the truth is in there."

I know it's wrong. Sally's half my age, and I'm not supposed to feel these urges. But I do, and she knows it. "All right. But stay back. They might've had some kind of disease."

Behind me Jerry's cousin Minnie tittered again. A soft scrunching of paper told me she'd plopped herself on the feedbags to watch the show. Another one Jerry owed me — as if that little rodent would ever pay up.

I circled the killing machine, crouching and stretching to examine the box from every angle — not an easy thing to do since I was still trying to avoid looking at its contents. Small brown stains, still oily and slick, caught my eye. They were far enough away from the box for me to risk hunkering down for a closer examination.

Sure enough, the spots smelled familiar. "Chocolate," I said. "That stuff's poison."

"No way! That's Godiva," Jerry protested.

"Muldoon has a point," Sally said. "Every diet doctor I've ever seen on television says chocolate's bad for you. Not only does it clog your arteries, it also acts like a happy pill on the human brain. But," Sally shot me an apologetic glance, "strictly speaking, unless you're allergic, it's only poisonous to cats and dogs."

"Do the dead guys look like dogs to you?" Jerry asked.

"No, they look like victims of the Jonestown massacre, and I can think of only three possible explanations for that. One—it was some kind of killer virus, and we're all going to die horribly in less than five minutes. Two—a serial killer… or alien," I added for Sally's benefit, "is using the box for his own private morgue. The problem with that is nobody looks like they were stabbed or shot or strangled or dissected. Nobody's missing any body parts. The only thing that supports the morgue idea is that some of the bodies look older than others, which means they didn't all die at once.

"Which means we have to explain why they all crammed themselves, one after another, into this box to die. It must've stunk to high heaven, and it's not like *The Guinness Book of World Records* has a category for most dead bodies in a confined space. So, what do we have left? Number three—poison or drugs, probably both."

Jerry's shoulders twitched up and down. "I dunno. They could've had their reasons. Me and Minnie used to play here as kids. Used to be a great ride—and free, too. Dead is dead, you know. Way we live, you can't let it get you down."

"Can't let it get you down?" Sally sputtered. "You mean you'd climb over a stack of decomposing corpses for a cheap thrill? What kind of ghoul are you?"

"Hey, it's not like there's anything else to do in this neighborhood," Jerry said.

Minnie's black eyes glittered in agreement. Some of the corpses had Minnie's drab coloring and almost the same nose and narrow cheeks. They might've been relatives, but that didn't seem to bother Minnie. Instead, Minnie swiped a hand across her mouth in a way that suggested she was getting hungry.

It's one thing to dream about investigating the paranormal and inexplicable abductions that happen to somebody else. It's quite another to discover a completely alien intelligence in your own backyard. Gives a whole new meaning to the phrase "trust no one." But Sally held her ground.

"It couldn't be poison," Sally said in a small voice. "One thing about the Boss, she wouldn't leave anything that could do this lying around where people could get into it by mistake. She even makes the exterminator use that insecticide made from chrysanthemums. Muldoon…"

She sounded so forlorn I would've done anything to make her feel better. If I could've given her aliens, I would've. If I could've faked aliens, even better. But all I could do was look the dead in the face and see if I'd missed anything the first time.

Still trying to keep the immediate area clear for the professionals, I crouched down as close as I dared to the open bay. No visible spores, no dried froth around the mouth, no obvious sores — good, good, and good. The body didn't even smell that bad. No worse than dried mushrooms anyway. Which probably ruled out poison as well as disease.

I forced myself to take in every detail. Nothing looked broken, but the way the body sagged made it hard to tell. Concave. Boneless.

So why was the corpse's arm still sticking in the air? I angled my head closer to the opening.

Damn.

I risked touching a knuckle to the crank. With a terrible groan, the drum lurched slowly, slowly, grinding and tumbling its contents together. I told myself Jerry was right, dead is dead, and they don't feel a thing. The almost invisible seam in the back of the bay widened, and the body slumped to the floor.

"Hey, it still works!" Jerry exclaimed.

"Unfortunately," I said. "But only partway. That's the problem. Your friends went in for a ride. They tripped the spring like always. But the mechanism must be rusted. It moved too slowly, and they got caught between the cylinder and the bay. And, once they got caught, there was no way they could get free. Look at the wrist on the one in the bay if you don't believe me. And it's worse in here."

"Oh, no," Sally whispered. "They starved to death trying to get free. What a terrible way to die."

"Coulda been worse," Jerry said philosophically. "Hey, thanks for looking into this. I wasn't worried, you understand, but Minnie's not so tough."

Minnie laughed uproariously.

"Muldoon, we've got to do something," Sally said. "It's our garage. We can't just let that thing sit there. More people could die."

"Nah, it's pretty full," Jerry countered. His gaze wandered, as if by accident, to the bin where the Boss kept the shelled nuts. "But as long as we're here, you mind if we grab a snack?"

Like I'd do anything violent with Sally around. "We shouldn't move the box or dispose of the bodies. We leave that to the professionals," I told her.

"And until they get here?" Sally asked.

"We wait. You don't believe in ghosts as well as aliens, do you?"

"Not really." But she snuggled close to me anyway.

The low, ominous growl of an idling motor woke me from a doze. The garage door moaned as it lurched upward, compelled by an unknown hand. The rumble of the motor swelled to a tornado's roar that consumed all other sound. Jerry and Minnie streaked from view. Scraps of paper, leaves, seed, and other debris flew in every direction, as if even the inanimate sought to flee the twin white suns rolling inexorably towards the trap.

I squinted against the glare, spots the shape of fat carp swimming across my vision. Sally buried her face in my shoulder. I felt the pulse in her throat throb against my chest.

"Sally, Muldoon, what are you doing out here?" the Boss demanded. She stopped in front of the still burning headlights of the Volvo and a made a grab for us. Then she saw the trap.

"Bad cats! Bad, bad cats!" The Boss wagged her finger at us. "Eek! What are all those dead mice doing there?"

About time she noticed.

"Most Dead Bodies in a Confined Space" was first published in Strange Pleasures 2, *Prime Books, 2003.*

Duzell

SHEEPDOG

An Alliance Archives Adventure

Mike McPhail

"Most of the people in our society are sheep. They are kind, gentle, productive creatures who can only hurt one another by accident. Then there are the wolves, and the wolves feed on the sheep without mercy. Then there are sheepdogs, and I'm a sheepdog. I live to protect the flock and confront the wolves."

Paraphrased from "Sheep, Wolves, and Sheepdogs"
Lt. Col. Dave Grossman

IT WAS A RELIEF TO FINALLY ESCAPE THE SMOTHERING DARKNESS OF THE old-growth forest. Its ancient canopy had long ago meshed to form an impenetrable barrier blocking the life-giving light of Tau Ceti's sun. Nature had not seen fit to give the planet a celestial traveling companion, as with Earth and her moon, so the term 'the dark of night' had a whole new meaning here.

As starlight shown on the scene through towering grasses at the edge of the tree line, the suit's all-governing computer, or Pacscomp, powered down the peripheral, infrared lamps, once again allowing the helmet-mounted, electro-optical scopes to gather the faint ambient light and amplify it into a false-color day.

The armor-clad figure pressed forward until the sea of grass parted like waves breaking against the bow of a ship. Visibility was less than a few inches, fostering a complex feeling of concealed safety and overt vulnerability as his passage created a hole in the surrounding landscape.

Navigating by landmarks was impossible, yet the scouts pressed on, guided only by the down-view overlay, which gave them an approximation of their position. As with all things deemed vital to the cause, both sides in the conflict had electronically fought for control of the orbiting constellation of LandNav satellites, ultimately rendering the system virtually useless. So it was the suit's digital compass, in sync with the transponder they had set up back at the insertion point that guided them this night.

"Slow it down," another spoke directly into his mind, the tone flavored by the adrenaline-fueled tension of the moment.

The scouts had been moving at a trot since leaving the bushes at the edge of the tree line. Without responding, the one in the lead down-shifted into a walk and focused on the map. Its scale indicated that they were about twenty yards from the parameter roadway, heading straight for a rock outcropping.

The sound of his breath opening and closing the suit's air-handling system was almost drowned out by the background noise of the winds dancing across the field, whipping the grasses, and creating a white nose reminiscent of falling rain.

Glancing over toward his comrade, there—superimposed against the wall of foliage—was a green, rounded-point triangle, topped with the letters RWL. Its relative size indicated that the scout was less than five yards away. The sight of his teammate's icon reassured him; it added a physical presence beyond just the comm traffic and the voices in his head.

"I'm telling you," his comrade continued the conversation they'd started earlier, *"she was up all day and night screaming and demanding my attention."* A feeling of being tired washed across the electronic commune.

"And...?" asked Ke'Se, trying to keep his amusement from being conveyed.

"And so I did as nature intended," replied Ra'Ewl with a hint of pride. *"But in truth, there's only so much enthusiasm before all that biting and scratching gets old."*

"You're a spaz for complaining," Ke'Se responded. "So, no nap then?"

The very top of the rock outcropping came into view, less as an image, and more of a void punched out of the starry sky.

"Just what we had on the flight in." Ra'Ewl slowed and then took up a position at the foot of the rock. Its surface was almost weathered smooth, but at least this facing sloped up to its summit at a traversable angle.

"Going right," stated Ke'Se as he crouched for a slow pass along the side of the rock. Now just a yard from the cleared edge of the grasses, he went down onto his belly. He spied the world through the last few inches of cover.

"Clear?" asked Ra'Ewl impatiently as he revved up for the leap.

"Standby." Ke'Se crawled forward and gently pushed his head through the grass, opening up the field of view to his helmet-mounted scope. To his front lay a swath of crushed stones that had been used to stabilize and defoliate the ground around the roadway. With a slow pan of his head, he scanned the area for any immediate threats.

"You're good to go."

"Going up," Ra'Ewl communed with an accompanying *hooff* over the comm as he leapt. The jump brought him to just below the grass tops. Gaining purchase on the rock took a little more than just the traction pads on his boots. With a snap he deployed the fighting claws and pressed hard against his toes. At a measured pace — as laid down by eons of evolution — he moved slowly toward the crest.

Feeling more like a gecko climbing out onto a rock to sun himself than a predator on the hunt, Ra'Ewl settled onto the high point and waited for the suit's equivalent of chromatophores to shift into a dark gray. *"I AM…the rock,"* he communed with a sense of playfulness.

After another quick sweep, Ke'Se pivoted to look up at Ra'Ewl, whose green icon floated ethereally at the back of his helmet. Despite the carapace plates that made him look like a child's toy robot, there was still no mistaking that he was fifteen pounds worth of cat, stuffed into AS'Is (Allied Standard Issue) body armor.

Although spawned from a thousand generations of domestic house cats, nature was no longer in the driver's seat. As the end product of the animal-experimentation phase for the Synaptic Interface — direct mind–machine communications, or commune — Doctor Jonathan Parr's feline lab rats took on an unexpected life of their own, as comrade-in-arms with their bygone tormentors.

From his perch, Ra'Ewl could see the town's parameter roadway, with its long, curving arc and accompanying sidewalk. There were no lights to be seen, only the myriad of road-designating phosphorescent reflectors giving up their stored energy to the night.

The town of Stratford was typical for Demeter, a bullseye layout with a series of concentric circular roadways and spoke avenues, dividing up lots. At its apex was the Administrative Centre, which housed everything that an isolated town of two thousand projected residents might need.

"Raul what is your position?" came over the comm in a slight Scottish accent.

Ra'Ewl's tail twitched at the thought of making mischief. "Standing on a rock," he replied over the comm via the commune, and then turned to look down at his fellow scout.

There was a pause. "Aye. Echo's status?" replied the voice from his helmet's speakers, asking if they had spotted any sign of the enemy, or Echo, from the phonetic alphabet.

"Still looking for those bad-guys." Both he and Ke'Se started to chirp with laughter.

Yet another pause. "Raul. Kizzy. Maintain comm procedures," instructed the voice. The letters OWN shown on the squad-ban display.

Ra'Ewl did a quick front stretch, and then reared up into a sitting position, all the time scanning for movement.

This isn't the first time Corporal Owens has expected us to play like soldiers, thought Ra'Ewl to himself. Being an expatriate of the Dominion, only Owens knew why he'd chosen to fight under Allied Military authority.

"Owens, the bad-guys can't pick up our comm traffic, and even if they could, they don't have the Pacscomp to translate it. That's why they're all hot and heavy to get their hands on one."

"Aye, I've been told all that, but I'm sure Donitz felt the same way about Enigma," quipped Owens. "So if you two are through pissing about, I need you to move onto the objective."

"Who's Donuts?" asked Ke'Se.

"Haven't a clue." Ra'Ewl leapt from the rock. *"On the move."*

The outermost ringed streets of Stratford were nothing more than a flattened bit of land, with yellow boundary lines and brass benchmarks proclaiming their future address. Many of the lots already had their poured foundation slabs and adjoining utilities trenches running out to the street. Just ahead, a picket of landscaping trees marked the boundary to the completed section of the town.

Ra'Ewl swung left at a trot, following the tree line with Ke'Se in tow. Through the thicket of screening foliage laid the boxy, two-story prefab buildings that were predominately used across the planet. No doubt each had been adorned by their owners to express their own personal idioms, but here in the dark they were just more oppressive, monolithic structures seemingly devoid of life.

"Ra'Ewl!" communed Ke'Se, with a sense of discovery.

The Parr looked back toward the construction zone. One of the slabs had a large piece missing next to a wide depression. As they approached, the ground they covered was awash in a spray of dirt and shattered bits of concrete.

"This is it?" asked Ke'Se.

Ra'Ewl had already turned and was looking about for others. *"Yeah I think so; it looks like two more over this way,"* he replied before heading off.

It took them a few minutes to arrive at the third hole; this one was in a patch of open ground. Ra'Ewl estimated that the crater was about two and a half yards across and a foot deep. He then noticed that Ke'Se wasn't looking at the crater, but back toward the house.

Ke'Se purred with fascination at a tree between him and the building. To say the tree was broken would have been an understatement. The crown had been blown off, leaving foot-long splinters sticking up at odd angles. The upper portion now sat on the ground, resting against the bole of the tree.

"Fell short," commented Ke'Se as he moved in for a closer look.

Ra'Ewl suddenly felt the need to get to higher ground, but the best he could do was a nearby pallet of building materials. It was piled high with polymer sacks, many of which were torn open and had hemorrhaged their contents. They were filled with some form of granular material. With a dash and a leap he landed on top and gave a good hard look about.

"Owens, from Ra'Ewl," he communed; now watching Ke'Se as he moved behind the devastated tree, to be replaced by just his floating icon.

"Owens, go ahead, Raul." the letters OWN brighten on the Parr's display.

"We're on station. Negative contacts. There are three confirmed hits, and a possible tree burst. The craters are the right size for the enemy's eighty-ones." he reported.

"Understood, what did they hit?"

Ra'Ewl had another quick look. "Nothing. They landed in the construction zone back behind the first street of houses." Ke'Se's icon was receding, heading off toward the nearby house. Ra'Ewl was anxious to join him.

"Roger that."

Ra'Ewl leapt from the pallet and darted off. "Owens, we say 'acknowledged' in this cat's Army," he communed, knowing that it would annoy Owens to be caught making such a simple mistake.

"Acknowledged," the human said in a taut tone. "Keep me informed. ETA about fifteen minutes, Owens out."

As Ra'Ewl cleared the trees, he saw that Ke'Se had crossed the backyard and was now just outside the building. Crouched down, he used the thickness of the back deck for cover. The storm door's clear, polycarbonate panels were fractured, and the inner door lay open and at an angle.

Ke'Se briefly looked over as Ra'Ewl settled in next to him. *"I'm getting a glow on thermal from somewhere near to front,"* reported Ke'Se. His display was showing him the world from his scope's far-infrared pickups. Everything was painted in shades of cold blue to white hot; the interior of the house was awash in warm colors reflected off numerous surfaces; it looked very much like a room lit by a fireplace.

"Big or little?" asked Ra'Ewl, as he slowly moved off toward the left side of the house.

Ke'Se checked the color-coded thermal key at the bottom of his display. *"Maybe around eighty degrees ambient, it's hard to tell without line of sight. Whatever it is, it's small."* he added.

"Like a monkey-boy has his helmet off?" Ra'Ewl was now just under a large picture window that faced out onto what appeared to be the homeowner's garden project. The cleared ground was edged with a continuous strip of black plastic, while underneath the window lay a neatly stacked pile of rock pavers.

"I don't think so; it's bigger than that."

Checking that the pavers screened him from the street, Ra'Ewl stretched up his full length; he was just short of being able to look into the window. *"Okay, be ready to run if someone spots me,"* he communed, almost excited by the possibility.

"Acknowledged." Ke'Se backed up so he could get a running start into his turn.

"Suit, scope up," Ra'Ewl commanded. A small insert window opened on his display. Its round image was almost fish-eyed, and clearly in motion. At the end of its extension, the flexible scope stood a foot over his head and parroted the movements of the helmet.

The space was a living room, decorated in a modular, out-of-the-catalog style, with two couches forming an L near the window. Across the room was a theater display, its flat-panel screen gouged, the frame missing pieces.

Tilting his head, he scanned the area along the floor in front of the seating area. There, partially covered by the far edge of the couch, sat a child, it was doubled over as if resting its head on its knees.

"Shit!" communed Ra'Ewl conveying a feeling of annoyance.

"Big shit or little shit?" misconstrued Ke'Se. Ra'Ewl ignored his attempt at being a smartass.

"Suit, scope down." The scout was on the move even before the scope locked safe into its housing. *"Back door, we're going in."*

Ke'Se was standing to one side as Ra'Ewl reached the storm door. Standing up on his hind legs and grabbing the knob with both paws, Ra'Ewl gave it a twist and reared back. As the door gapped, Ke'Se intervened and shoved it open with his body.

Cautiously, Ke'Se peered around the edge of the inner door. Nothing had changed. They entered the room slowly; its floor was covered in rough tiles and was lined with counter tops and appliances. To the right was a staircase.

"Check the second floor," ordered Ra'Ewl.

As Ke'Se went for the stairs, the hot spot came into view through a myriad of chair and table legs.

Ra'Ewl could feel his comrade's concern. *"Go check for bad-guys,"* he ordered.

Quietly Ke'Se climbed the stairs as Ra'Ewl lowered himself into a stalk and moved to get a better look. It seemed that he had been too distracted by the sight of the child to see the truth of the situation. Lying there, just on the other side of the dining room table separating the living room from the kitchen, was a body. Ra'Ewl didn't bother with a biometric scan, if the human had been among the living Ke'Se would have seen that on thermal. *"Anything?"*

"Negative. On the move."

Ra'Ewl stood up and walked toward the child, swinging wide to avoid the body and the pool of congealed blood that surrounded it. Looking back he could see that Ke'Se had just turned the corner.

Together they stood in silence and pondered the scene. The child was a small female, dressed in a long-sleeved T-shirt and overalls. Her head rested forward against her knees, and her long hair draped to the sides of her black, rubberized field boots. One arm was up underneath her, holding some form of plush animal, while the other hung down; its hand was gripping the hair of the adult. It too was female.

"Suit, thermal disengage." He turned to face Ra'Ewl. *"Mom?"*

Ra'Ewl didn't answer what he felt was obvious. *Things are getting complicated*, he thought to himself, as he looked around in the hope that an answer to this problem would just materialize if he looked hard enough.

In a sense it did; while he was distracted, Ke'Se had moved to within just a foot of the girl and was reaching out to touch her leg.

"No stop that, bad Parr, don't…"

Ke'Se had stopped as Ra'Ewl barked the order, but with paw outstretched, the scout stood frozen in the moment as the girl looked up. Her eyes were dilated against the darkness, and through his night vision scopes they shown as bright as a cat's. There was just a momentary pause, as confusion washed across the girl's tear-stained face and her young mind raced for an answer.

He had just lowered his arm when tremors shook her body, and the girl screamed. Involuntarily he leapt, flinging himself back almost a yard. Ke'Se landed with a padded thump, back arched. The comm was now awash with primitive emotions, as the sounds of his hissing and growling flooded the channel.

Ra'Ewl fought to maintain his composure. *"Ke'Se, stand down!"* he ordered, while trying to drive across the feeling of being in control.

Ke'Se wound down as he watched the girl desperately trying to backpedal away from him, only to be stopped by the edge of the couch.

"Just great, get over here," demanded Ra'Ewl; the girl's voice was strained, as if she'd already given as much as she could to the effort. No longer screaming, she trembled with fear, while clutching her stuffed animal.

As Ke'Se moved passed Ra'Ewl, he pressed himself against his comrade's side asking for forgiveness, resulting in a series of thumps as composite plates smacked into each other.

"What were you thinking?" The tip of Ra'Ewl's tail flicked with annoyance.

The image of sitting on the floor and playing with his friend's children hung in Ke'Se's mind. *"Mac's kids always liked it when I patted them,"* Ke'Se communed defensively. In the early days of the Project, Dr. Parr had isolated and switched off the gene that created the cat's claws, making his front paws more like prehensile hands than weapons, and thus safe for playing with children.

"Yeah, but here and now, all you are is a Jonathan-forsaken monster; just a shadow against the dark." Ra'Ewl paused, as if hearing his own words being spoken by someone else. *"Get out of your suit,"* he ordered.

"What? Are you spazzed?" The very thought clearly panicked Ke'Se.

"Just do it." Ra'Ewl looked around to see how much cover they had. The windows had no blinds or curtains, so they must have been the type that electronically went opaque.

"Why me?" argued Ke'Se, as he assumed the position.

Ra'Ewl looked for the main controls; odds were they were somewhere near the master's seat on the couch across from the theater display. He moved with all the stealth he could muster, while watching the girl and hoping that he didn't frighten her any more than he already had. *"Because, the monkey-boys gave me an AS'Is hair cut to deal with the suit's tactile contact points, whereas you are still fuzzy,"* he communed with a sense of amusement over his partner's growing distress.

Lying on his stomach, Ke'Se moved his front paws to either side of his helmet. With a firm push, he depressed the twin latches; the backpack portion of his armor popped opened. Arching his back, he pulled his head free, leaving his helmet still connected to the suit's neck coupling.

Over the commune, a wave of disgust hit Ra'Ewl, who was almost to the couch. Turning so he could see Ke'Se's head, but his ears were back, and he had one paw over his nose, as he had seen the humans do in such a situation. *"The smell…"* Ke'Se trailed off.

"Deal with it; we'll have a Vettech give you a bath when we get home." At the moment the girl was distracted by the sounds of Ke'Se extracting himself from his armor. Ra'Ewl leapt for the couch; there, built into the padded armrest, was the controller. With a stubbly digit he pressed the window-screen button. In an instant, the stars no longer shown through the panels, as the dark became black. The girl gasped in horror and started sobbing.

"The batteries still work," he mused as he turned to face the scene. Ke'Se was out of his suit and standing in front of the child. *"Ready?"*

Ra'Ewl asked, before realizing his mistake. The Pacscomp could only communicate with the user's Synaptic Interface within the confines of the helmet.

"*Suit, external,*" he instructed. "Hi there." sounded the male-neutral voice from the Parr's external speakers. The girl turned toward the voice; her eyes wide; her mouth hung open as she panted to breathe.

"It's okay, we're here to help. Don't be scared." It sounded cliché. "*Suit hold, lights, thirty-percent, maximum diffusion, engage.*" The helmet's side lamp came on. Even at its low setting it still came on like a blazing sun. Ra'Ewl's night vision switched off.

The girl squealed and raised her arms to cover her eyes against the light, the blue plush animal she had been holding dangled precariously by its long ears; a trail of white stuffing leaked from its midsection.

Ke'Se had guessed his comrade's intentions and was prepared. Slowly, he opened his eyes, allowing his pupils time to constrict. The girl's boots stood like a grime-splattered wall in front of him. Not wanting a repeat of her earlier reaction, he decided not to reach for her, instead he purred.

Timidly the girl peered around her arms in search of the sound. Her blue eyes locked onto Ke'Se's, who then squinted his eyes in greeting and tipped his head slightly to one side to be cute.

For the first time something less then terror shown on the girl's face; slowly she unfolded herself and tentatively reached out toward the black-and-white cat. Ke'Se stepped forward, thrusting his head under the girl's hand and pressed into her palm.

To Ke'Se surprise, the girl giggled nervously and rocked forward onto her knees to throw her arms around him in an effort to pick him up. Of course, at fifteen pounds he was easily over a third of her weight, so he just stood there, as she hugged him and buried her face into his soft fur.

"Raul from Owens, status!" came in over the comm. "What's happened to Kizzy?"

Ra'Ewl paused for a moment to figure out what to say; no doubt Ke'Se's icon fell of the grid once he was out of range of his Pacscomp. "Ah, we have a domestic situation here," he answered.

"Be more specific."

"We found a child in the house near the tree strike," he replied, wondering what would happen next. Looking up, he could see Owens' icon in the distance.

"Standby. I'll be with you shortly," he instructed.

Sighting in on the scouts' icons, Owens entered the building, closing the damaged door behind him as best he could. The Parr's small helmet lamps lit up the house as if it were high noon. Owens went down on one knee, using the counters for cover from the windows; his weapon was at the ready. "Raul, turn them off." The house went black; the intensity of his night vision display rose to compensate. The false safety of the darkness returned.

Staying low, Owens moved over to the body. Next to it, the girl had reared back trying to take Ke'Se with her. The Parr—now standing up on his back legs—was held tight as if he was the girl's only hope. Lowering his weapon, Owens allowed it to hang across his chest by its strap.

"Raul?" he commed, as he reached for the body. Firmly he grabbed it by the shoulder and moved it; it was cold and sluggish, but not stiff. *Whoever she was, she's been dead for more than a day*, he surmised.

"Raul…" he repeated, when he realized that the Parr was sitting next to him. "Did you check their RF tags?" he asked, looking over at the girl. A knot now gripped his stomach. He'd seen that look of terror before, and not on the faces of a stranger, but of a friend, long ago, when her own parents had met a similar fate.

"Negative, I don't have a reader," communed Ra'Ewl, as his suit's synthetic voice joined in.

With a practiced hand, Owens reached into his side pack and retrieved a wallet-sized device. He then held it near the body. "Suit, RF scan." With that command, an ID photo and data line appeared with an arrow pointing at the body. Her name is—was—Sherilyn Carter; it went on to list that she was married and had a daughter.

Owens then aimed the reader at the girl. "Christine 'Crissy' Carter," he read aloud over the comm; "Year of birth, 2059. She's only three." Owens fought to keep his emotions in check.

"Did you find anyone else?" he asked, wondering about the father.

"Nope."

Owens gently reached over and put his hand on Mrs. Carter. Silently he prayed. He then took a deep breath; it cleared his mind and helped steady his emotions.

He then reached into his pack and pulled out a disposable chemlight. Removing the safety cap, he depressed the igniter, which popped.

As the chemicals mixed, the room became awash in a soft white glow.

"Sheeet." meowed Ke'Se in Purrsing, the closest thing the Parr had to a spoken language, as Crissy clutched him in a death grip when Owens was revealed by the light. Clad in his AS'Is carapace armor, the soldier must have looked like some form of unimaginably large insect, suddenly materializing out of the darkness. Crissy was frozen in fear.

"It's okay, he's not going to hurt you, he's a friend." said Ra'Ewl in an effort to comfort the girl.

"Easy, easy…" Owens commed before realizing she could not hear him. "Suit, external." "Easy there, sweetie," he said, calmly leaning forward, and motioning with his hand. Clearly it wasn't working. Owens was still some faceless monster in her eyes.

"Suit, unlock." he said as he reached up and pulled the mandible portion of his helmet free. In response, the visor raised, leaving his face framed by his comhood. "It's okay, sweetie, please don't squish the cat. They're expensive," he said gently.

Ke'Se's tail swished with annoyance at the remark, but at least the girl calmed down.

"Raul, you get Kizzy back into armor," Owens said as he stood up and walked toward the kitchen, then up the stairs.

There was no sign that the girl was going to give him up. Ra'Ewl knew Ke'Se could fight his way free, but the scout would never consider doing so, even as a last option. Longingly, he turned to see what his comrade was up to.

Ra'Ewl was now next to them reaching for the girl's discarded plushy; his glove's prosthetic grippers were deployed and acting as a set of opposable thumbs. With the toy in paw, he moved off in a three-legged hop, to sit down with his back toward the two.

Owens had returned; his helmet was closed with the visor still up. He was carrying a small blanket adorned with wide-eyed blue bunnies. "What's the hold up?"

"Working on it," Ra'Ewl said. Turning he held up the plushy as he closed his medpack; the rabbit's torn abdomen was now covered by a gray contact bandage. He gently shook it, making its long ears flop about.

"It's okay, sweetie, you can take your rabbit," Owens assured her.

Reluctantly, she let go of Ke'Se and grabbed for the toy. She clutched it even tighter than she had the cat, all the while giving Owens and Ra'Ewl a pouting frown, as if their handling of her toy was more of an offense than their presence. Ke'Se backed away the moment she took possession of the plushy.

"Right," Owens said in a firm tone. "We're going to EVAC her to the recovery site."

"What about the mission?" asked Ra'Ewl, as he helped Ke'Se back into his armor. "Couldn't we just leave her here, and pick her up on the way out?"

Owens knelt in front of her; setting the blanket aside he reached over and placed his hands on her upper arms. "Can't take the chance. If something happened…" he trailed off. "Besides, we've accomplished the primary objective, so everything else is 'up to the discretion of the team'," he quoted.

"What if we leave Ke'Se here to keep an eye on her?"

Ke'Se was mostly back into his suit, with only his head still sticking out. "Feek que," he meowed, and pushed his head down through the neck coupling. Ra'Ewl then flipped his backpack closed, and like a man doing CPR, he pressed down onto his comrade's back with both paws, throwing his weight into the effort.

"On line," communed Ke'Se, as he flipped his head around while trying to get his paw up to his faceplate as if trying to groom. *"Damn, I stink."*

Owens angled his head, both Parrs' icons shown on his display. "You two, outside, check for Echoes," he ordered.

Ke'Se tromped off in compliance; Ra'Ewl sat down next to Owens. "You know she's going to shine like a marker beacon in the infrared."

"No shite," Owens agreed. "All we can do is dampen her down and break up her silhouette."

"What about telling… someone she's here?" said Ra'Ewl reluctantly; he'd expected Owens to spaz out on him for even suggesting turning her over to the bad guys; the Legion.

"That's not happening, cat," stated Owens, a determined edge to his voice. "Now get outside and do your job."

"Acknowledged." Ra'Ewl ran from the living room.

Owens turned to look at Crissy; she was so very small, his armored gloves were massive by comparison. It would be so easy to unintentionally hurt her. "Sweetie, I need you to stand up, can you do that for me?" he said while nodding his head in the affirmative.

On shaky legs she stood. Owens helped to steady her, but in the back of his mind the fear that he might accidentally break her fought for his attention. Carefully he retrieved the blanket and placed it around her so that it could be pulled up over her head.

"Mommy!" Crissy cried in a hoarse voice; tears welling up in her eyes as she uselessly flung herself hard toward the body on the ground.

Owens held on to her, knowing too well that if she didn't calm down, this was not going to work. All he could think to do was fall back on what had comforted him. "Crissy, sweetie, please look at me."

Her tear-filled eye met his. "Sweetie, we have to go. Mommy is with God now, and I promise you, that after you have had a long and happy life, you'll be with her again." Owens' faith had always been strong, but in this day and age, God was often something other people talked about, not something they believed in.

It could have just been the look in Owens' eyes, or his sincere tone of voice, but Crissy stopped crying and fighting him. She closed her eyes and clung to him as if what he'd said had changed everything.

Relieved, Owens swung his weapon so that it rode under his right arm within easy reach of his hand. Snapping closed his visor he gently picked up the girl and carried her on his left arm, the thumb of that hand tucked into the webbing of his load-carrying gear. "Raul, Kizzy, status?"

"All clear," they replied.

"On the move."

The team moved through the darkness as if it held no domain over them. Once again they were operating on active night vision, as their infrared lamps punched small arcs of scenery out of the surrounding void. The Parrs were scouting ahead. Owens followed, trying to minimize bouncing the girl around as he negotiated the uneven, root-covered ground.

"Hold up!" instructed Ke'Se, excitement flavoring his words as he went to ground.

Ra'Ewl went down onto his stomach.

Turning off his helmet lamps, Ke'Se sat up. Ra'Ewl looked off into the same general direction to see what had attracted his comrade's attention. With his lights out, Ra'Ewl crept up on Ke'Se and then slowly sat up next to him. *"Where?"*

"At about thirty-degrees, something moved against the ambience of the clearing."

Through Ra'Ewl's scopes, the break in the trees shone like sunlight as seen at the far end of a dark tunnel. *"Suit, nine-power."* His display transitioned into a magnified view; now the slightest movement of his head was exaggerated. Looking down at his compass display, he aimed his head to thirty-degrees.

Intently, he scanned the area. There it was; a rounded, smooth shape, black against the background glow. It was moving to its left, toward another of its kind standing next to a tree. The silhouette was all too familiar.

"Owens, we have bad guys!" Ra'Ewl communed, not waiting for Owens to confirm he was listening.

"Raul, say again!"

"We have ECHOS between us and the recovery site!" repeated Ra'Ewl, making sure to emphasize the term Owens used for the bad guys.

Owens darted for cover behind a bank of surface roots. Like gigantic snakes they twisted around and over each other, covering the ground between the two massive trees. Bracing the girl with his free hand, Owens came to an abrupt halt behind the roots; going down onto one knee, he leaned forward so that only his head was above the edge.

Startled, Crissy cried out.

In the still air of the forest, the sound carried; bouncing off into the distance.

The Parrs turned in response; Owens icon was at the epicenter.

Ra'Ewl swung back to reacquire the bad guys, things had changed. "Owens, the Echoes are on the move."

"Roger that," replied Owens. He turned to the little girl.

"Sweetie, please quiet down," he pleaded, his helmet just inches away from her. No good. "Kizzy, get back here. Raul, maintain contact, and make damn sure you don't get between us and the Echoes," he ordered.

Pulling the blanket up around her head, Owens carefully placed the girl down into a gap among the roots. "Crissy, you need to stay here," he told her. She was already trying to work her way free. Owens used careful force to keep her in place.

Ke'Se landed with a soft thump, his IR lamps on low barely lit up the scene; Owens was always astonished at just how fast a Parr could run. "Suit, external, disengage." He was now back on comm traffic only. "You keep her here anyway you can." He gestured for Ke'Se to take over. "Knock her down and sit on her if you have to, just keep her under cover."

The Parr moved around Owens' legs, and up under his arms; with outstretched paws he took over. "How do I keep her quiet?"

Owens moved back and reached for his weapon. With one smooth motion he brought his square-framed rifle up and placed it at the ready. On his visor's display the weapon's semicircular targeting reticle appeared, its PIP (Projected Impact Point) dot resting at its center. "You don't." He then moved off.

"Ra'Ewl, what do we have?" Owens moved quickly to gain distance from the girl.

"Two, possibly three Echoes, moving toward your..." Ra'Ewl looked back, Owens' icon was moving up off to his right. He corrected his response, "Ke'Se's position. They're just over a hundred yards ahead of me."

"Stay left and close to fifty. Then bunker down."

"Acknowledged." Ra'Ewl sped off.

Owens was still covering ground, all the time looking for an advantageous place to set up his ambush. "On station," came over the comm from Ra'Ewl. *The time is now*, Owens thought. Just ahead was another ancient tree, its trunk easily six yards across, with massive surface roots splayed out from its buttress.

He moved into position behind the tree. Looking around, he tried to memorize the position of the potentially foot-tripping roots. With his left hand against the tree, he turned off his IR lamps and maneuvered around the trunk.

Now in relative darkness, he could see the distant glow from the far-off clearing; Ra'Ewl's green icon shown off to his left. Intently, he scanned the arc between himself, the Parr, and the clearing. His eyes locked onto two sets of small lights. A sudden feeling of intense anticipation washed over him, not unlike a child forced to wait to open a present.

Bracing himself against the tree, he raised his weapon. With a squeeze of his right hand, he depressed the leading edge of the rifle's handgrip; *Click*. The safeties were off, and power made available. A pull of the two-fingered trigger would now launch a salvo of electromagnetically accelerated armor-piercing darts.

Owens settled his sight's PIP onto the further of the two. "Firing!" he warned his comrades over the comm, as his darts cracked through the air, breaking the sound barrier. The first target bounced from the hits, but without waiting for it to drop he swung onto the second. He couldn't hear the concluding thump of his projectiles as they punched through mesh body armor to render flesh and smash bone, but he knew with satisfaction they had hit.

He released the trigger and the world went quiet, nothing moved. Owens took in a breath; he had been holding it while he fired. Although it had only been a few seconds, his body demanded air.

"On the move," called Owens as he stepped forward over the root. He'd heard the *thump* and caught sight of the flash; in that moment, his training took over as muscle memory tried to drive him to safety.

Everything was a blur of motion as the world flew past at strange angles; memories of being in the heart of a blazing fire raced in his mind. He could hear breathing, it grew louder and labored, his eyes snapped open; it was him.

"Status," he choked. Coughing, he spat up something; it had a strong metallic taste.

"Corporal Owens, you are critically injured," stated the Pacscomp in its emotionally neutral female voice.

Owens fought to reorient himself; he was prone and lying on his left side. As he kicked out with his right leg, a wave of pain slashed through him. The momentum rolled him onto his back, the pain forcing his eyes shut, trapping him in hell. "Combat!" he screamed past the pain.

"Corporal Owens, the administering of Comburodorphin in your current state could result in exsanguination," it said calmly.

"Do it!" he demanded. The threat of bleeding out from the Combat drug seemed meaningless.

The initial sensation of the transdermal spray hitting the base of Owens' neck was lost to him. Then the drug reached his brain, and the pain faded away. It felt like cool water ran through his vein, as the drugs' synthetic hormones and endorphins dominated his body. His eyes dilated in response, and his mind finally cleared.

"Ne se deplacent pas!" someone yelled in French.

Owens could feel his heart pounding in his chest, as his reality shifted into slow motion. He looked up; there just on the other side of the surface root stood a Legionnaire. A bullpup assault rifle pointed at

Owens, the mercenary's hand gripping the weapon's underslung 30mm grenade launcher.

"Don't move!" the gunman restated in English.

Something was moving fast at the edge of Owens' display. Like some mystical creature of the forest, it seemed to fly through the air toward the enemy. It was Ra'Ewl's icon. With a *thud*, the scout connected high on the mercenary's back, knocking him forward over the root, toward Owens.

Startled, the mercenary pushed out his left arm in an effort to break his fall; the assault rifle still held by its pistol grip in the other.

Owen reared up to meet him; making a desperate grab for control of his opponent's weapon, he did manage to shove it aside as the gunman landed on top of him. Now as the tide of battle shifted, Owens wrapped his left arm around the mercenary's neck and grabbed for the back of his equipment harness, pinning his face down onto Owens' chest.

Panicking, the mercenary fought to bring his legs up under him in the hopes of pushing free.

Owens held tight as he threw his own leg across the captive's. He then grabbed for his knife, and with a *snap*, pulled it free from its sheath. With a hard thrust, the thick blade's reinforced chiseled tip punched through the mercenary's mesh armor and sank deep into the side of his throat; his whole body jerked as the edge struck home.

Like a vise, the mercenary locked his hand onto Owens' knife-wielding arm; desperately he pulled at his tormentor. Owens knew it was just a matter of time; he could feel his captive's strength failing, as fingers lost their hold and went limp. With a twist, he pulled the knife free to an accompanying gush of arterial spray. A sensation of warmth was conveyed across his gloves' tactile contact pads; blood continued to pump from the opening.

"Tae the Devil with ya!" yelled Owens as he pushed the still-twitching body of the mercenary aside; it rolled over and landed with a *thump* onto its back, bending its right arm at an unnatural angle and trapping the assault rifle underneath.

Owens turned to look for his own weapon; it lay just a few feet away tethered to him by its strap. Planting his knife in the ground, he reached out, his fingers closed around its roll-bar hand guard. He pulled the rifle into his arms and made it ready.

"Owens?" said a familiar voice. Standing on the chest of the fallen mercenary was Ra'Ewl, his head darting about as he attempted to take stock of the situation.

Owens took a deep breath, something wasn't right. "Yeah, I'm with you."

Ra'Ewl lowered himself down onto his belly, seemingly to get a better look. "Your left thigh is a mess. Can you walk?"

Owens knew the answer. He placed his gauss rifle on the ground and then patted his chest. "Come here."

Ra'Ewl paused for just a moment, then stood up, walked over, and settled down onto Owens, who was now reaching into his side pack. Owens placed his hand on the Parr's backpack, where he then flipped up a small metal loop and held it in place. In his other hand was the connector end for the emergency carry strap, which if need be, he could use to sling a Parr like a piece of equipment; it *snapped* as he hooked it into the ring.

"Get her to the recovery site."

Ra'Ewl stood up and climbed carefully up toward Owens' face. There he stood for just a moment, as if he could see in through the helmet's frontal armor. "*Roger*," he replied, then turned and headed off.

Owens sat with his back against the tree, his gauss rifle across his lap. The damage to his thigh was horrendous, but he did what he could. He'd used up the medpack's coagulant spray in an effort to slow down the blood loss and now only a pressure bandage kept him from bleeding out. Tingles ran down his neck as the suit administered drugs to help keep him stable.

"We'll be on the ground in less than fifteen," stated an unseen voice. "Just hang in there."

"Roger that." Owens closed his eyes; the suit had lowered its internal temperature to an uncomfortable level to buy its user a little more time. He could feel his hot breath blowing past his cheeks. There was a glow beyond his eyelids, something was flickering.

He struggled to open his eyes as he turned his head; arm muscles twitched in an effort to raise his weapon from his lap, but to no avail. About ten yards away was a moving pool of white light; through his scopes it blazed like a searchlight. Owens smiled. Ra'Ewl had turned on his helmet lamps, and with Crissy in tow holding tight onto his carry handle, he was guiding her through the darkness. She stamped along behind him in her oversized boots, while holding her blue plushy rabbit high up under her left arm.

"I know how you feel," joked Owens, remembering the contact bandage that Ra'Ewl had put across the rabbit's soft belly.

Ke'Se was just behind them; he stopped and looked in Owens direction. An unspoken sense of kinship seemed to pass between them. Owens raised his hand and motioned for Ke'Se to keep moving. At a trot Ke'Se caught up with the others.

Once they had gone, he was alone in the dark; the sounds of comm traffic from the approaching ADF tilt-rotor aircraft played in the background. His mind started to wander; it had found its way back to Crissy's house, and the sight of her eyes wide with terror. Owens looked over at the dead Legionnaire, then thought about the other two he'd taken out, and nodded with satisfaction. "Now there are three less wolves."

"Sheepdog" was previously published in By Other Means, *Dark Quest Books, 2011; reprinted in* The Die Is Cast, *eSpec Books, 2017; reprinted in* By Other Means, *eSpec Books, 2025.*

Kismet (Ke'Se)

TNR (TRAP, NEUTER, RELEASE)

WHILE WE WOULD LOVE TO SEE EVERY CAT IN ITS OWN HOME, SAFE AND sound and taken care of, the honest truth is that is in no way possible. There are way more cats out there than there are homes to put them in. And that aside, for most cats born in the wild, with no hint of domesticity, such intervention is unwelcome and in most cases doomed to fail. The older they are, the more opportunity they have had to develop a distrust of humans.

If kittens are caught early enough there is a good chance they can be socialized and placed in a good home, and older cats who are friendly and receptive to people could fostered and possibly adopted, but generally feral cats are trapped, neutered, and then released back into their territory where they have already made a niche for themselves.

TNR is a long game. While it can help with population control, its true goal is to improve the situation of those feral cats returned to the wild. Not only does it help prevent the birth of more ferals, but neutering has significant health benefits. First, female ferals are not subjected to an unending cycle of pregnancy and birthing kittens in unsafe conditions. Second, neutering of males and females relieves the constant pressure caused by reproductive hormones, which leads to less aggression and territorial behavior, such as spraying, fighting, and yowling. Third, there are a number of diseases linked to reproduction, such as cancer, that are then prevented.

When cat communities are reported, volunteers either set up humane live traps or actively act to trap the cats in question. The cats are then taken to a vet where any existing medical conditions are treated and the animal is neutered and vaccinated. They are then either put into foster if they are reasonable candidates for adoption, or, if they are health enough to release, one ear tip is snipped to alert future rescuers that the cat has already been neutered, and they are returned to where they were captured. If that area is deemed unsafe, they may be relocated as barn cats or moved to another area. This can be risky, however, as there could be conflict with any ferals who have already established territory in the new location.

In addition to the health benefits to the cat, the process of TNR alleviates overcrowding in shelters and avoids the possibility of the cat being put down due to that overcrowding. If you need to report a cat community near you, please contact a rescue or shelter that practices TNR.

CAT FUTURES
Lawrence M. Schoen

I believe that every short story author writing fantasy and science fiction has a list that they must check off before they're done. They must write a cat story, a vampire story, a poker story, a story set in a bar, a story set in a bookstore, a story involving time travel, a story that ends with a shameless pun, and so on. This is my cat story.

I'D ONLY BEEN DATING AMY A COUPLE WEEKS WHEN SHE ASKED ME THE question that changed everything. It happened in a coffee shop a couple blocks from campus. She'd just come from an art history class and sat warming her hands around a double mocha grande with extra whipped cream, waiting, as I finished reading the last few paragraphs of a novel for English Lit.

The minute I closed the book she pounced. "So, Steven, are you a cat person?" She's like that, no build-up, just right to the point. A refreshing change from the kind of girls I usually dated.

We'd met at the campus health center. Friends had brought me in after I'd landed hard on my head during a game of supposedly touch football. She was there having some prescription filled. The first time I saw her, she seemed surrounded by a glow of light. Okay, it could've been part of being smacked in the head, but at the time I just stared at her like I was seeing an angel. Then she turned, and her eyes caught mine, and the next thing I knew I was introducing myself to her and asking her out.

And now, two weeks later, she was asking me about cats.

"What? Well, I guess. I mean, sure, I like cats. I don't dislike cats. I've never had any though; we always had dogs when I was growing up. And my little sister had a rabbit once."

"You're talking about pets," she said. "I'm talking about cats."

"Yeah?" She still had that glow. I couldn't see it anymore, but I could feel it.

"Cats aren't pets. They're autonomous beings that sometimes choose to share their lives with you."

"Cats aren't pets?" I took a sip of coffee. Not a latte or an espresso, just ordinary coffee. That's the kind of guy I am.

"Well, okay, *some* cats are pets. But that's like some people are dumb, you know? Like some people go through life as drones, no imagination, no creativity, no ambition. So, yeah, some cats are like that, there are drone cats. Those are the ones that are pets. But the *real* cats, they're special and they're smart and they are most definitely *not* pets."

"Do you have a cat?" I asked. I'd never been to Amy's place, but I knew she had an apartment somewhere off campus. Like I said, we'd only been dating a couple weeks, and on the few occasions we ended up somewhere, it had always been my dorm room.

"I don't *have* one, but there's a cat who came to live with me three days ago."

I smiled at that. I'm not sure why, but it sounded cute to me. So many things about Amy struck me as cute. "What's her name?"

"I can't pronounce it. It's in cat talk."

"Cat talk?"

"The language of cats. Not the pet kind, the real kind. And he's a he, not a she."

"Well, if you can't pronounce his name, what do you call him?"

"I call him Mr. Buttons. But he says his name in cat talk translates more closely to 'Traveler Amidst Shadows of Possible Destinies.'"

She said it with a totally straight face, and I had to fake a sneeze to keep from laughing out loud. When I'd recovered, I asked, "Why is that his name in cat talk?"

"Because," said Amy, "Mr. Buttons can tell the future."

"How do you mean?" Don't get me wrong, I had real feelings for Amy, but this was starting to go from silly to weird, and you only have to date one really weird girl to get a little gun-shy about it.

"He knows things," she said. "Things that are going to happen."

"Right," I said. "And he tells you these things?"

"Steven, don't be silly. Cats can't talk."

"Then how does he—"

"He uses the words on the refrigerator. Those magnetic poetry things. You know, individual words that you rearrange to make a haiku or sonnet when you're putting away the milk."

"And the cat does this? Puts the words together in different ways to tell you the future?"

"Yep. He's only been doing it for the last few days. I haven't told anyone else. You're the first."

"Why me?" I asked, not sure if I meant it rhetorically or not.

And then she smiled, and I felt that glow again. Yeah, I was smitten.

"Because Mr. Buttons told me to. He wants you to come see him. He says there's something about the future you need to know." She looked at her watch. "Do you have time now? I'm all done with classes for the day."

We finished our coffees, and I followed Amy to her car, my boots crunching through the snow. We drove to the older section of town, about as far from the university as you could go, to a small collection of apartment buildings that had probably looked shabby back when they were new, and they hadn't been new since my parents were in diapers. A shining blanket of snow makes a lot of buildings look nicer; it didn't help here. Amy pulled the car into a parking lot and stopped in a numbered space. We got out and I followed her through a rusty gate and up two flights of stairs. Her door had three locks.

The apartment was pretty small, a studio with a bed that folded down out of the wall. Amy had a desk and a bookshelf and nothing else in the way of furniture. Instead of a kitchen, over in one corner there was a dorm fridge with a little microwave stacked on top. A sliding glass door on the wall opposite the front door opened onto a tiny balcony that held a pair of green plastic deck chairs, a litter box, and a basket of cat toys. The apartment was little more than a cracker box, but even so, it was nearly twice the size of my dorm room, and she didn't have to share a bathroom. The place looked shoddy, but Amy shone there, like a fairy-tale princess who couldn't stop being a princess even though she'd been sent off to live with evil peasant stepparents in a thatch hut by a tulgey wood.

"So where's the cat?" I asked.

"Mr. Buttons likes sunning himself on the balcony. I'll go get him."

I did a slow circuit of the apartment while Amy went to fetch the cat. Then I did it again. It was a really small apartment. She came back in with an enormous orange tabby cradled in her arms. She tickled him under his chin and murmured nonsense syllables to him.

"Here, you take him," she said. "I'll set up his word pieces."

Fumbling, I took the cat. "I thought you said he used those fridge magnet things."

"Yeah, but he doesn't do them on the refrigerator. I keep them in a cardboard box on the bookshelf. Here you go." She set a shallow box on the floor; the kind of box your aunt uses to send you a Christmas sweater. Inside were hundreds of white plastic chits with words printed on them.

"How does this work?"

"You clear a space at one end of the box. Then Mr. Buttons uses his left front paw to pick the words he wants and pushes them into the right order."

"Why the left front paw?"

"That's the paw of prophecy," Amy said, staring into my eyes, her face suddenly solemn and serious.

"Paw of prophecy?"

"It's the one that only has four toes."

I shook my head. "I'm missing something, I think."

She paused, and her voice dropped to a near whisper. "The future isn't spoken or written. It must be four-toed." She paused, like she'd just revealed some holy truth, and then her lip started quivering and she broke up in laughter. "Ha! Got ya. There's nothing to it; Mr. Buttons is just a lefty." She giggled again. "A south paw."

I rolled my eyes theatrically, which just made her laugh more. What can I say? My girlfriend likes bad puns. But although she'd been joking about why Mr. Buttons used his left front paw, she was still serious about the cat's abilities.

"Okay, I'm going to leave you guys alone for a bit while I go get my laundry out of the basement."

"What am I supposed to do with Mr. Buttons?" I said.

"He's going to tell you your future. He's fussy, though, and doesn't want me here when he does it. But don't ask him too many questions, I'll only be gone five or ten minutes."

She blew me a kiss as she walked out the door and pulled it shut behind her. I set the cat on the floor, and he immediately lumbered over to the cardboard box and began moving chits around with his left front paw. After a moment he looked up at me, rather expectantly I thought, or as expectantly as a cat can look I suppose.

"Sure, Mr. Buttons, I'll play." I pushed the chits around in the box until I'd cleared a small space. The cat had pulled his paw back while I did this, but as soon as I finished he plunged in, flicking word chits this way and that. Then, just as quickly, he stopped, backed away from the box, sat back on his haunches, and stared at me. I looked into the box. Six chits had been lined up in the open space:

I WILL TELL YOU THREE THINGS

I looked at the words for a full minute and then looked at the cat. He flicked his tail from side to side, rose to his feet, and strode back to the box. Once again he moved words with his left front paw. When he finished, he backed off again. I looked into the box.

YOU WILL MARRY THE GIRL IN TWO YEARS

"Oh really? C'mon, we've only gone out a few times. She's special, and I like her a lot, but that's crazy. Oh hell, I'm arguing with a cat. Maybe *I'm* crazy."

Mr. Buttons cocked his head and pronounced a very clear "Mrowwr." Then he moved back to the box and went at it again. When he finished this time he pulled his paw from the box but didn't back away. He tilted his head and looked at me, as if daring me to look at the second of his three pronouncements.

THE GIRL IS IN DANGER UNLESS YOU HELP HER

"Danger? What kind of danger? You're freaking me out, cat." I got up from where I'd been kneeling alongside the box. I went to the sliding door and out onto the balcony. I needed air. This was just too much. I liked Amy, I liked her a lot. Sure, maybe in time I might even realize I loved her, really loved her, not just the smitten, infatuated feeling I had for her right now. But, there was something seriously wrong here. Her cat foretold the future? What was up with that?

After a bit, Mr. Buttons followed me out onto the balcony and began doing that cat thing where they rub back and forth against your legs. When he had my full attention once more, he turned and walked back inside, back to the box. He didn't put his paw inside; he just sat down next to it and glanced up at me.

I came in and knelt by the box again. The cat had already laid out the third message. I read it and just stared for a while, trying to take it all in.

THEY GAVE HER THE WRONG MEDICINE

I stood and went into the bathroom. It was the kind of tiny bathroom that you'd expect with a tiny apartment, and it had the standard mirrored medicine cabinet over the sink. I opened the door and found what I was looking for, a small plastic, amber vial from the health center pharmacy. I took out my cell phone and called the phone number on the vial.

They answered on the third ring. "Campus pharmacy."

"Hello, I'm calling for Amy Saunders with regard to..." I checked the label. "Prescription number 3821964."

"I'm sorry, sir, I can't discuss another person's medications without her permission."

"Yeah, okay, but I just want to make sure she's got the right pills. You can call up the prescription on your computer, right? Are the pills supposed to be blue?"

"Blue?"

"Yeah, light blue, with a runnel down the middle so you could snap them in half."

"No sir, that's not right." The voice paused. I imagined the pharmacist on the other end of the phone biting her lip. "Are there any markings on the pills?"

I spent the next few minutes describing the pills in detail, reading the full label off the vial, and then promising to take Amy to the health center immediately.

She returned with a basket of folded laundry just about the time I was closing my cell phone. She still had that same glow about her, just as when I'd first met her.

"I'm back. What did Mr. Buttons tell you?"

"I'll tell you all about it in the car," I said, though I knew I wasn't going to mention any of it. Not then, maybe not ever.

"Where are we going?"

"We're going to the health center, and you're going to let me drive your car. You've been taking the wrong pills for the last two weeks. You could be delusional, or worse, you could start having seizures."

"What are you talking about? Is this a joke? Did Mr. Buttons put you up to this?"

I took the laundry basket from her and set it aside and gathered her in my arms. "It's going to be okay. Another week, and it could have been very serious, very bad, but the pharmacist said you haven't been taking it long enough to do yourself any permanent harm. C'mon, I'll drive."

And that's what I did. When we got to the health center, they took Amy into an examination room and confirmed what Mr. Buttons had told me. They said they needed to keep her there for a few days to flush the drugs out of her system. She'd be fine, barring some slight memory loss.

I promised Amy I'd take care of the cat until they discharged her, and the look of gratitude on her face made me glad I'd done so. But when I went back, I couldn't find him anywhere in the apartment. He was just gone.

The box of word chits, though, was on the floor where I'd left it, along with a parting note:

TOSS MY STUFF I'M DONE HERE

Mr. Buttons, a.k.a. "Traveler Amidst Shadows of Possible Destinies" had moved on.

I still didn't want to believe in a cat that could order me around with word chits, but that ship had long since sailed. So I gathered up his food dish, litter box, toys, and any other evidence that a cat had been in the apartment. As I carried everything down to the dumpster, I tried to make sense of it all. Why had Mr. Buttons told *me* Amy was in danger, instead of just telling her himself days earlier? Hadn't that put her in more danger? I still couldn't understand it.

When she came home a few days later, Amy didn't say a word about the cat foretelling the future. She didn't remember ever having a cat, and when I asked her, she laughingly told me to stop teasing, because she'd always wanted one, but her apartment building didn't allow pets.

I attributed it to the memory loss and dropped it. I couldn't explain what had happened, or how, but it didn't matter. Amy still had that glow about her, and I was still smitten. We kept dating, and my feelings for her only grew deeper.

It took a couple months before I finally realized the obvious truth. Mr. Buttons hadn't come into Amy's life to save her from pharmaceutical incompetence; he'd come to bring us together. I still didn't have an explanation, still didn't understand how it had happened, but when I looked at Amy I could see my future. And I no longer needed a cat to spell it out for me.

"Cat Futures" was first published in The Town Drunk, *2006; reprinted in* Sweet Potato Pie and Other Surrealities, *Hadley Rille Books, 2010; reprinted in* Sweet Potato Pie and Other Stories, *Paper Golem, 2018; reprinted (in Chinese) in* Cats Non-Exist, *Hunan Literature and Art Publishing House, 2020; and reprinted in* Hellcats, *Magpie Lane, 2020.*

Shiloh and Karma

FEROCIOUS ANGEL
Rigel Ailur

"WHY," ELIZABETH HOLLINGSWORTH SHOT HER CREWMATE AN incredulous look as the elderly woman trudged up the gangplank, "did you wait so long?"

Locks of the septuagenarian's snow-white hair kept falling across one eye, and she'd twist her mouth to blow them clear. She didn't have a free hand to brush them aside. At the moment, Eleanor affected none of the frailty she feigned to garner sympathy, and deflect suspicion, in her advanced years. She needed all her strength and coordination to keep her grip on the struggling white and gray feline in her arms. The cat yowled in displeasure.

"Took me this long to catch her. You thought it would be easy?" Eleanor raised her voice over the cat's protests and pointed with her chin. "Open the door."

Eyebrow raised, Liz opened the door to the captain's quarters, then closed it quickly behind the woman. A few crashes and bangs sounded inside, punctuated by growls, howls, and the occasional hiss.

Good thing Coventry liked cats.

Sighing deeply, Liz stood at the bow of the shallow-bottomed riverboat *Menace* with its double mast and sail and fought the urge to leap into the gently windswept water. The feline wails faded quickly.

She hated this part. She always hated waiting.

The gentle breeze barely created ripples across the river's surface as it danced over it and through the lush, green treetops. Brilliant sunshine dappled the wooden deck of the boat as if in a playful tug-of-war with the shadows cast by the low-hanging branches.

The glorious spring weather mocked her sour mood with its bright joviality and vernal pulchritude.

Logically she understood that Coventry wanted someone trust-worthy and responsible — such as her, his second-in-command — looking after matters until he got back. She still hated the crew being separated in these dire circumstances. Moreover, she loved the little village and The Dancing Fish, the inn where she and the rest of the pirate crew could always find refuge.

But now their presence endangered the townsfolk.

A cold, hard smile touched her lips. The most recent blow they'd struck against the sheriff made their sacrifice well worth it. They'd ransacked the local sheriff's treasury and had rescued thirty people due for execution. Amazing — and a huge shame, Liz thought — that the murderous sheriff hadn't died from apoplexy.

An added bonus: they'd gotten the king even more furious with the sheriff. The king could oust the man from office at any time.

They could only hope.

Coventry had insisted on going by himself to the depths of the forest. He'd needed to warn one of their allies about their impending departure. saying the farmer who often sneaked them food would not believe any other messenger and besides, he wanted to say goodbye to his old friend.

Liz had acquiesced to that. Neither particularly difficult nor risky, the job didn't really require more than a single person. Yet she hated for any of her people to go solo. Far better to have backup near at hand. Besides, none among them were more recognizable than Coventry.

The wanted posters of Coventry actually looked like him. They showed a man with a pleasant enough yet unremarkable face, blue eyes, and dark blond hair. The picture didn't show his average height, of course, nor did it capture the humor perpetually sparkling in those kind eyes. He had an appealing, gentle manner that evoked trust and drew people to him. His eloquence inspired people to follow him — and to protect him and his crew.

Her wanted posters made her look twice her twenty-five years and — despite showing just the face and shoulders — somehow still made her look like a hulking amazon. Maybe it was that they'd inaccurately drawn her features even rougher and larger, the shoulders too broad.

Liz didn't mind in the least that the authorities had no good likeness of her. Better for her to have gone on the errand instead of Coventry.

Eleanor darted out of the cabin and secured the door behind her.

"What?" she demanded in response to Liz's sidelong look. "You know Ruffian is a good hunter and earns her keep just like any of us. She'll keep the mice and rats out of our cabin, protect our food."

"I know. It's not Ruffian. I won't be able to relax until Coventry's back."

Eleanor nodded sagely. "Any time now. Then we can get going. It'll be good to catch up to the others."

"Definitely."

Of the twenty in their pirate crew, normally ten stayed on the boat. Another twenty or so had assisted them so blatantly that they needed to flee as well.

In groups of two or three, four at most, they'd set off over the past week for the other side of the kingdom. The trickle, instead of a mass exodus, hopefully would not draw attention. So long as they received their money and goods in taxes, the upper crust paid no attention to the lowly peasants.

Liz and her friends just needed it to stay beneath their notice for a little bit longer.

Coventry returned shortly before nightfall, right as *Menace* prepared to shove off. The riverboat glided away from shore, its two sails unfurling and snapping taut as they caught the night wind. The crescent moon followed them downriver. Its delicate silvery light didn't overwhelm the glittering sea of stars overhead.

With a wave of his hand and tilt of his head, Coventry gestured for Liz to follow him to his cabin. She trailed after him, grinned as he inched the door open and peered inside to see if the coast was clear. He slipped quickly inside.

She followed his example, carefully shutting the door behind them. The compact room had a bunk, with drawers above and below it, built into the left wall. Windows made up the top half of the far wall. A table and two chairs sat to the right. A lantern on the table cast flickering shadows around the small room.

It also illuminated a pair of glowing gold eyes from the deep gloom of the inset bed.

Coventry picked up the cat, who promptly purred and rubbed all over his face and neck as he sat down.

Liz took a chair at the table. "Sounds like our new house is set," she said. Then her face clouded. "But we have too much coin there.

We'll need to distribute it as fast, and as discreetly, as we can. Otherwise..."

"I know." Coventry stroked Ruffian, who purred loudly in appreciation. "Soldiers find that there, and we'll be running again before we've even stopped."

A young man, powerfully built as one would expect of a blacksmith, met them on the dock which led right to the back door. He spared a nod and smile for Coventry carrying the feline inside before enfolding Liz in a hug and kissing her soundly.

After a few minutes, they followed inside. Liz chuckled at the ongoing inspection.

Ruffian stalked around the big, open room, thoroughly examining it to see if it met her requirements for comfort. The stone floor and crude, yet sturdy wooden furniture evidently failed to impress her. She showed more interest in the cheery fire blazing in the huge hearth and in the robust aroma of a succulent stew cooking in the huge cauldron inside the fireplace.

After sniffing a few times, the cat padded over to a large rocking chair with a blue and green Afghan flung over the back. She pawed the blanket until it fell into the seat, kneaded it into an acceptable cushion, then curled up in the middle of it.

A ladder in one corner led up to a common sleeping area overhead. Eleanor and several of the other women and men in the group had already retired for the evening. Coventry sat at a long wooden table eating a bowl of the stew. He'd set two more bowls out as well.

"The coin?" Liz asked, sitting down eagerly to the hot meal.

"In the chimney wall. Some brick was loose. You have any trouble, John?" he asked the young man.

The blacksmith scowled. "The sheriff wanted a repair on a gate. Wasn't difficult, but it made me hours late. Seemed safer than telling him it would take until tomorrow and having him annoyed and notice right away I was gone."

"You don't think he suspected, do you?" Liz asked, heart suddenly in her throat on his behalf.

"No, and I want to keep it that way."

"Wise decision." Coventry nodded in approval. "No use being too obvious."

They fell silent as they savored the rich beef stew, full of plenty of chunks of meat and copious potatoes and other vegetables. Eschewing wine or ale for the evening, they got water from the bucket used to draw it from the well.

Tension finally began to ebb as they relaxed in relative safety.

"You going back to *Menace*?" John asked as they all sat content after the hearty warm meal.

Coventry chuckled. "Of course." He glanced around the big room in satisfaction. "This'll mainly be our meeting place of last resort. You and your 'mother' Eleanor — and Ruffian, naturally — can keep it looking lived-in and maintained."

"It'll take a few days to get set up," Liz said to Coventry as much as to John, "but they found a good place deeper in the wood for our camp. And that cove across the river is perfect to hide *Menace*."

"It'll still be good to stay hidden for a few weeks, and get a better feel for this new area," Coventry said. "Figure out what the authorities are like here, what their schedules are."

Liz snorted. "Not that they'll be any different."

The trio exchanged sad looks of agreement.

"At least there are a few villages close enough I can get blacksmith work, once I get a forge built," John said, his optimism sounding forced to Liz's ear. "And lots of people can use a good seamstress and weaver. Eleanor will have options if she wants to keep busy."

Liz shot him a wry glance. "You mean when she's not practicing knife-throwing?"

John laughed. "Of course."

"It will be good for the two of you to be able to show how you get your money." Coventry couldn't hide his own smirk, though.

Few people messed with Eleanor more than once. No one in their group handled knives better.

Liz folded her arms and leaned against the doorjamb as the last of them — Coventry and John — boarded the dinghy to cross the river. She'd 'guard' the house, not that they expected trouble, while the rest of them gathered for the meeting to confirm the ground rules of their new territory.

They'd need to take great care to find out whom they could trust, and whom to avoid — or beware of.

A renewed pang of longing for The Dancing Fish stabbed at her gut. It would take a long time for them to find that level of security again.

Back inside, Ruffian had claimed what looked to be her favorite place: the rocking chair by the fireplace. With nothing cooking at the moment, and no need of heat on the temperate spring day, they'd let the fire go out. Better to save the firewood for when they needed it.

The smoke, soot, and ash had done its additional job: hiding the fact that sections of brick had recently been removed and replaced.

Without the fire or the lantern lit, deep gloom pervaded the cavernous room. Her eyes already adjusted, Liz could see just fine, but the small windows let in so little illumination that someone entering from the bright sunshine into the dimness would be temporarily blind.

Suddenly, Ruffian raised her head, tail twitching and a growl deep in the small feline's throat. With a hissing snarl, she leapt down from her chair, raced across the room, and using her momentum, sped up the ladder in the corner to the loft.

Liz cursed.

Now what?

Could anyone possibly have followed them there? She didn't believe so, although she forced herself to consider every possibility.

She stood perfectly still, but didn't hear anything aside from the wind rushing through the leaves outside, and the river gently lapping the bank.

After just a moment, she heard hoofbeats. From several horses. Not traveling particularly fast.

Even so, that couldn't be good.

A bunch of horses together usually meant soldiers.

She could follow the cat and pull the ladder up after them. She rejected that option a split-second later. Soldiers could still get up there easily enough, and it had no other exit.

Grabbing her bow and quiver of arrows from beside the door, she ran outside away from the incoming riders, and into the woods. Blinking at the sudden brightness, her eyes watered.

Just as she climbed high enough to hide herself in the tree branches, four magnificent gray war horses, soldiers in chainmail astride, trotted into the clearing between the house and the river.

The four men, all of the same type, dismounted in unison and tethered their mounts to the well. Tall, burly, two-handed broadswords on their left hips, identical neatly-trimmed beards and moustaches.

Even had they not been wearing mail and the colors of the king, everything about their deportment screamed 'soldier'.

Liz held her breath as they strolled around, realized she was doing so, then took a slow, careful breath.

"Looks like someone really did move into this haunted old place," the oldest of the quartet said as he eased the door open with his sword. The years had roughened his deep voice.

Gray touched his brown hair lightly. He could have been any age from forty to fifty, but the other three — their faces unlined where their beards didn't cover, like their foreheads and cheeks and the corners of their eyes — didn't look older than their early twenties. And they moved without the stiffness their — Liz guessed — commander was just starting to succumb to.

The younger three gathered behind their leader and all four peered into murkiness.

Liz's crewmates had given the place a thorough cleaning. No more dirt, grime, or cobwebs. Clearly, lived in. The solders would see as much if they went in.

She held her weapon ready in case they saw her, knowing full well that the very last thing she should do was kill any of them. The river pirates needed the authorities to stay away, or, at the very least, to ignore the place, not swarm all over it or stay there in search of whoever had attacked their comrades in arms.

Her heart sank as the four men trooped inside.

Her friends had left nothing of any particular value or interest sitting around. And she felt confident they'd never find the coin. But if they decided to loiter there, she and her people would have nowhere to go. They certainly had no interest in meeting the local military.

"What's that?" the man's voice echoed weirdly in the stone building. "Is that eyes?"

"Where?" the deeper-voiced commander replied.

A keening yowl, at once angry and mournful, emanated from the building. What the heck was Ruffian doing? Hadn't she stayed hidden up in the loft?

"There!"

"Where?"

"Look out!"

"What?"

Startled, not-quite-simultaneous shouts overlapped, accompanied by ungodly shrieks that only an enraged cat could make.

A metallic thud told her they'd upended the cauldron, and it was rolling around. A more muffled bang sounded like the table and benches falling over and being shoved across the stone floor. Metal met stone with sharp clacks as blades connected with the floor and walls. The four soldiers stumbled out of the building.

Wide-eyed, Liz needed all her effort not to laugh out loud — as that would surely have gotten her killed. Their mail hung askew, revealing the shredded non-chainmail material of their jerseys and pants. Blood flowed from deep gouges on their hands and faces.

They stood looking at each other in the clearing, as if unsure what to do next. Their horses whinnied and neighed, their equine anxiety plain as they pulled at the reins tethering them near the well.

"Wolves," the youngest soldier finally said, stroking the neck of one of the steeds.

"A mother wolf defending her cubs," a second chimed in as he gathered his own roan mount's reins.

"A pack of wolves," the third suggested. His gray mare attempted to sidestep away, but the soldier kept a firm grip on the reins and a comforting hand on her withers.

Mouth twisted in annoyance; the commander gave all of them a hard look. "A pack of wolves," he confirmed. "We ran them off; they won't be a danger. No need to hunt for them."

The quartet all nodded in agreement as they climbed back into the saddles.

Liz still battled mightily to contain her laughter as they rode off. After the sounds of hoofbeats faded away, she clambered down from the tree and dashed inside.

Her eyes needed to adjust as she looked wildly around for Ruffian. Liz liked her and would never want anything to happen to her. Eleanor loved her dearly and would personally kill anyone who'd laid a hand on the feline.

Liz didn't want to face Eleanor if something had happened to Ruffian on her watch.

The cauldron lay on its side across the room from its hearth. All four chairs were scattered about, two of them broken. The upended table leaned against one wall. The ladder, also broken in two, had skidded across the stone floor as well.

Only the rocking chair had escaped unscathed. The chair, and the smug white-and-gray feline kneading the blanket on its seat. She meowed a coupled times at Liz then curled up.

Risking disturbing her, Liz hurried over and picked her up. Not a mark on her. Squirming as usual, Ruffian seemed to be moving just fine. Totally unhurt.

Liz gave her a quick hug and kiss and set her back on the chair. Affronted, Ruffian kneaded the perch again then settled back in.

Grinning, Liz began cleaning up the mess. *Thank you, Ruffian.* Their territorial feline had just added immensely to the house's reputation as a place to avoid.

Well done, little cat.

"Ferocious Angel" was previously published by Bluetrix Books in 2019 in The Angel Cat Collection *and is also available for sale as a single.*

Duchess

YOU TRY TO DO THE "RIGHT" THING
Danielle Ackley-McPhail

IT IS NO SECRET THAT I AM A SOFT TOUCH. MOST OF MY CATS HAVE BEEN scooped up from the streets and given a cushy home where we have in every way spoiled them, from a teeny kitten rescued from a tire, to a persistent orange boi who squatted in our alleyway for a week before my mother-in-law unbent enough to let us bring him in. I cannot see a homeless cat without wanting to help it, particularly when it has clearly chosen me.

But you know… that has gotten me in trouble in the past. I was very strictly told at one point I was not allowed to bring home another cat. I endeavored to listen, truly.

And what happens? A very small tuxedo cat comes running down the street to greet me. More than once. Like… almost every day. Sweet and playful, and not beyond climbing up onto my back so I couldn't catch my train for work until rescued by a neighborhood child. But I resisted, playing and petting, but leaving the little guy to roam.

So don't you know that got me in trouble. I told my husband about the funny little cat and the first thing out of his mouth was, "Why didn't you bring it home?!"

Turns out our little tuxedo had been greeting Mike as well.

Apparently, I was supposed to know there was an exception to the injunction on acquiring more feline friends, when clearly it was "meant to be."

As often happens in cases like this, the moment I had permission, the little bugger vanished. For two whole weeks I watched for him and nothing. Not until one day when making my way home from work, I stopped to do a good deed.

On my route home I regularly passed the home of an elderly couple that might well have been a glimpse of my future. They were unloading their car and struggling with large bags of litter and food. One bag had been left on the curb so I scooped it up and brought it to their door. Of course the conversation wandered to cats and how they had thirteen of their own and just couldn't take in another one. That is when fate struck.

The woman looked at me with a hopeful look and said, "Would you like another cat? We have a little one we take care of but just can't bring in." She then looked down at her feet and twining around her ankles was my little tuxedo.

I laughed and said, "Why yes I would!" and told her my story as I scooped up my newest baby—who came to be known as Kismet—and took him home.

Kismet

BODEGA BARRY
Marc L Abbott

I

"They took another one this afternoon," Louis Perez, owner of Perez Grocery and Deli, said to his friend Julio as he adjusted the candy display in the window. "That's got to be, what, five in under three weeks."

"Someone got something against gatos, amigo," Julio Ramerez said. He peered out the door. "This neighborhood is really losing its charm."

"Losing? It's pretty much gone." Louis stood and leaned on the counter. "It's that blonde that's behind this. I know it. She's been running some kind of campaign to get rid of the cats around here."

"You don't know that for sure." Julio turned and looked at the cover of the Daily News newspaper. "You see they found another victim not far from here? She'd been missing for nearly five days. They found her in the basement of her apartment building. Can't believe they can't catch this guy."

"They're not looking for him," Louis said. "That's at the gentrification border. If it happens here then they will look for him."

"Crown Heights? That's gentrified. I think this guy is just too slick." Julio flipped through the paper. "They can't…"

The front door opened, catching both men's attention. A Caucasian man walked in, wearing a long duster and a dark suit without a tie. He fixed his gaze on Julio who was staring at him.

"Hey," he said.

"Hola," Julio said.

Louis and Julio watched him as he checked the place out, stepping in further and tilting his head to peer under the stand holding the chips.

"Can I help you?" Louis asked.

"Hm?" The man turned to him. "Oh, sorry, I was just… you have any cigarettes? I need a cigarette."

Louis nodded and the stranger approached the counter slowly.

The smell woke him. A subtle, but putrid aroma that drifted through the bodega. Barry jumped down off the top of a box of condensed milk, stretched, then tipped his head back. He took another sniff and yowled. The cry caught the attention of the owner Louis, who was attending to a customer at the counter.

"What you crying about now, Barry? All you do is complain," he said with a slight Dominican accent.

Barry glanced at him then turned his attention to the man at the counter buying a pack of cigarettes. A stocky white man, clean-shaven wearing a duster. He had a chiseled face and sunken eyes. Not a familiar face in the neighborhood. Barry fixed his gaze on the man.

There was something not right about his aura. An indifference. He didn't look threatening, but he felt… cold.

The man didn't look at him. He fussed with the packaging and when he got it open, he quickly took a cigarette out and asked for a light. Louis pointed to a lighter hanging by a string near the door.

Henry held the cigarette up. "You don't mind if I? My name is Henry, by the way."

"Not at all. Nice to meet you."

Henry lit the cigarette. Taking a long drag, he expelled the smoke into the air. Then, without looking at Barry, he pointed at him with the cigarette.

"Bet he's hungry," Henry said.

"This good-for-nothing ole cat, all he does is eat and sleep. Good mouser though. Will catch and get rid of anything not welcome in here. Right, Barry?" Julio chuckled.

"You named him Barry? That's an interesting name."

"It was my uncle's name. Cat looks almost like him," Louis said

"Had him a long time?"

"More like he's had me. One day he just walked in here, found himself a spot, and we've been together ever since." Louis winked at Barry.

"They are a New York staple. Although I haven't seen too many bodega cats in this area," Henry said. "They're everywhere in Spanish Harlem."

"So you don't live here?"

"No, I'm here helping my friend, Drew Beckford. Working on updating an apartment in one of the buildings he owns. 519 St. Johns."

Louis gave him a blank stare. "We know Drew. You know a woman was attacked and died in that building."

"I heard. That's the apartment we're working on flipping."

"That's messed up," Julio chided.

"Well, I don't want to sound cold or anything but, what else are we supposed to do with it? Can't keep it empty for too long."

Before Julio could respond the door opened. In walked a Caucasian woman in her mid-thirties, with dirty blonde hair down to her shoulders. She sported a conservative black dress and a pair of Hip Optical round reading glasses which she pushed up to the bridge of her nose. There was an unpleasant look on her face, as though she had eaten something that didn't agree with her. She pulled an over-the-shoulder pochette that sat near her hip around to the front and opened it. As she approached the counter, she waved the air in a futile attempt to clear the cigarette smoke before her.

"So, you allow people to smoke in here too?" she said as she took out her phone and checked the screen. "That's a violation you know."

Louis' eye narrowed as she came closer. "What do you need, miss? I'm not in the mood tonight."

She looked at Henry. "Can I help you?"

"Nope," he said with a slick grin.

"What do you need, miss?" Louis said.

"My name is Casey, not miss." She put a twenty-dollar bill on the counter. "Give me two of the Altoids." Her eyes caught Barry's then she glanced at Henry. "You're a creep."

"I'm not doing anything," Henry said.

Casey looked at Barry. "Why is he looking at me like that?"

"Leave my cat alone." Louis placed two small tins of mints on the counter, took the twenty and made change. "He's not bothering you."

"He's a health hazard. There's a law about cats in stores," she said.

"That old law needs to be taken off the city books at this point. Nobody cares or even pays attention to it," Louis scoffed.

Casey glanced at the mints. "The cat hasn't been laying on these too has he?"

"He's a bodega cat," Henry said, catching a stern look from Casey. "Chances are he's been everywhere in this place. They protect the store you know. Keeping the undesirable away. Just think how this place would be if he weren't here."

An uncomfortable silence hung between them. Henry took a drag on his cigarette and blew a thin haze into the air above her head.

Barry meowed, breaking the quiet. All eyes fell on him. He stared at the woman.

She turned, grabbing her mints and her change. "Pets belong in a home not a store. That's where that cat should go."

"He's not a pet. You should be happy we have him. With all the vermin you people have brought to this neighborhood from wherever you came from," Julio said.

"Excuse me?" She took her phone from her pochette, held it up, and took his picture. "I'm reporting you."

Juilo half-laughed. "For what?"

"I'm reporting you about the conditions of the store, the cat, the fact that people smoke in here. I'll make sure they shut this place down by the end of the month."

"Oh, please," Louis said. "I've been in this neighborhood for forty years. No one's shutting me down. Make your little complaints. They know me downtown."

Casey turned and took several more pictures then pointed to Barry. "You're next!"

She stormed out, paused just shy of the door to put her things in the pochette, then walked away.

Barry saw her get on the phone as she crossed the street headed to the train station. He blinked and looked at Henry. The man watched her as he took a slow drag. Barry didn't like the way he stared at her and, to get his attention, he yowled. Henry turned quickly to him. Their eyes locked. Barry sensed anxiety coming from the man which started out as excitement but morphed into something more sinister. On instinct, he growled.

"She doesn't like cats." Henry took another drag from his cigarette. "Something about them being shifty and untrustworthy."

"Cats are a good judge of character, which is probably why she doesn't like them, and why she's been running around getting them banned from stores. They see right into her black heart," Louis said as he shrugged.

"Or maybe, just like many of these gentrificadores, they just want shit their way. They took everything else, might as well take the cats," Julio said.

Henry stepped away from the door just as another young lady walked in. She smiled wide and greeted Louis warmly saying, "Hola, Louis. Como estas?" Barry's attention quickly went to her. She was one of the many affectionate humans that came in regularly.

"Mia, hello, my dear, how have you been?"

"I'm good. Always nice to see you."

"Likewise. What can I get you?"

"I'm grabbing a water." She dug in her pocket and placed a dollar on the counter. "Where's your buddy?" She turned to Barry. "Hey, Barry, c'mere boy!"

Barry quickly approached, meowing as he lifted his head. She knelt and grazed her fingertips between his ears. He purred as she ran her fingers and hands over his body. Arching, he walked in circles so that she could pet him all over. He then fell onto his side so she could get his belly. As she did, he closed his eyes and flexed his claws.

When he opened his eyes, Maya and Henry had locked gazes. A look of apprehension shown on her face while Henry took a long drag off the cigarette with a lascivious expression. Maya exhaled and Henry breathed deeply. She coughed.

Sensing something was wrong, Barry hissed. That got Henry's attention. They locked eyes. Barry growled.

Maya placed her hand over her chest and started to inhale as though she lost her breath. "Woah, sorry. Lost my breath for a minute," she turned to Louis. "Such a good cat, but he's getting fat. Don't let him get too big. Remember what I told you."

"I know. I won't, Mia. You okay?"

"Maya," she laughed. "You'll get it one day. And yes, I'm fine." She turned back to Barry and finished giving him his rubdown. "There you go."

Maya stood and went to the refrigerator to get her bottle of water. Barry watched her, his tail swishing side to side from happiness. On her way back, he stood and meowed. She pet him on the head as she passed.

"I'll see you, Louis."

"Hey, you be careful out there. They never caught that guy attacking women around here. That creep could be anywhere," Julio said.

"Hey, you want someone to walk with you?" Henry asked. When he saw the uneasy look on her face he quickly said, "To see you safe to your building."

"Uh, thanks but I don't know you and I'm certainly not letting you know where I live."

"I wasn't trying to find out... I was just trying to be helpful that's all."

"Yeah, no. That's just..." She looked at Julio, concerned.

"I'll walk you." Julio gave Henry a disapproving look. "You better not follow us."

Henry put up his hands. "I'm not going to follow you. I wasn't trying to be creepy. My apologies."

Maya turned back to Louis. "See you, and I'll be careful out there. See you in the morning for my usual." She looked at Barry. "See you, Barry."

Barry watched her and Julio leave then he looked at Henry who was looking at her the way he had Casey but there was something extra on his face. A sinister grin. He started to move his lips, talking to himself as he nodded. He glanced at Barry. The grin faded.

"She's beautiful. I can't believe I messed that up," Henry said.

"Yeah, well, you were a little out of pocket there. Got to learn how to approach women better than that," Louis said as he stepped out from behind the counter. "'Scuse me. I need a water."

Barry tracked Louis with his gaze until the man passed by then quickly turned his attention back to Henry. The putrid stench that had woke Barry clung strong to the man. Barry groaned as the scent stung his nostrils. His tail twitched as his predator instincts kicked in. He had smelled this kind of odor before. From stick-up men, abusive boyfriends who lashed out on their partners in the store, and racists who moved in the neighborhood and got loud with Louis. It was the stench of evil.

A terrible energy emitted from the guy. Barry could also hear something sinister in the air. A whispering voice but it wasn't Henry. He noticed Henry's attention focused on Louis but another face that overlapped his stared down at Barry. Contorting to a twisted combination of horse and goat combination with white eyes.

"What a sweet soul. We must have her." the soft, sinister voice said.

"I want her too," Henry muttered.

"Stop drawing attention to yourself." The second voice snarled at Henry as Barry hunched into an attack position. *"Mind your business, cat. Her soul is ours. All souls will be ours to feast upon. And this area is ripe for the taking. Look at you, ready to fight. Well Barry this filthy human is our vessel. We have no desire to leave him to deal with the likes of you. We're not*

coming out. We need not to feed. So whatever you're thinking right now, forget it. You don't stand a chance against us. Your humans will die.

The face sank beneath Henry's and the man took a step forward.

Barry's ears flattened back as he snarled and growled and hissed. His back arched as his fur stood on end and his claws unsheathed. He set back low to the floor, planted his hand legs, shook his hind end then lunged forward. He drew his right claw back and swiped at Henry, who fell against the door in retreat.

"Barry, stop it!" Louis yelled.

Crying out in fury, Barry swiped again and sent Henry stumbling out onto the street. Barry started to charge just as Louis scooped him up and attempted to calm him.

"What is the matter with you? Stop," Louis said.

Henry got to his feet, glare at Barry with hate, then ran away. Barry writhed in Louis arms, and scratched him on the hand. Louis jerked his hand away, losing his grip on Barry, who landed out on the street. His shrill yowls filling the night as he ran out onto the sidewalk and looked both ways. There was no sign of Henry. Letting out a frustrated meow, Barry looked again before scurrying under a parked car. From there he looked up and down the street then sniffed the air, hoping to get the scent. But a light breeze robbed him of that.

II

Henry listened to them talking within his body as he walked in the direction Julio and Maya had gone. He stayed on the opposite side of the street where he would not be noticed, but keeping them in view as they walked a half a block ahead. He glanced back a couple of times to see if Barry followed.

"Why did you make this human back away? I could have taken Barry," the demon Impa said.

"That one is a fighter. Very aggressive. I could not risk the human getting scratched or I would have to untether myself from him. And then that would force you out and into harm's way," the demon Blasphemy said. *"You concentrate on getting us fed. I will worry about controlling the human."*

"I should get the man instead. Get him out of the way then let me handle the girl," Henry said.

Henry's muscles seized up, sending jolts of pain down his nerves with each step. He felt a pulling inside, like a teamster tugging the reins tight, that made him stop walking. He stood frozen on the sidewalk.

"You will do no such thing. We are in control. You do as we command. Her soul smells sweet and what we want. We have no care for the old man," Blasphemy said.

"We are losing sight of them. Deal with this behavior later. I need her soul."

Henry felt the grip on his body release. *"Move or our deal is done."*

The blood drained from Henry's face. "No, please, you can't do that to me. I'll keep up my end of the bargain. I need the work. And to satisfy my urges without guilt."

"You're falling behind the girl. Hurry before we lose her."

Henry picked up the pace until he saw them stop before a tenement. He watched as Maya and Julio hugged then she walked up the short set of stairs. Julio waited for her to take out her keys and enter. Unlocking the front door, she waved and stepped in, closing the door behind her. Julio returned her wave then headed back the way he came. When he was three parked cars away from the building, Henry darted across the street and pressed his body against glass in the door. He removed a pair of latex gloves from his back pocket and slipped them on then gripped the doorknob and turned it. The door was locked. He could feel one of the demons moving within. He put his head on the glass. The demon exited his body, passed through the door and within seconds the lock clicked. Henry tried the knob again and the door opened.

He stepped into the vestibule and was greeted by a second door with a square window at eye level. He peered inside and saw Maya getting her mail. He waited. Admiring her as she flipped through the small stack. He felt the presence of the demon, ice cold, brush past him and unlock the door. Henry carefully turned the knob, paused as the demon rejoined him and waited until she turned her back to head to the stairs behind her.

Now the fun begins.

Henry opened the second door, ran quietly up behind her. Seizing her around the waist with his left arm, he covered her mouth with his right hand. Maya screamed into his hand, dropping the mail and grabbing at his arm. She pulled but the demons within gave aide to his strength. Henry gripped her tighter and pulled her fighting to the back of the hallway and under the stairs.

He pressed her against the wall, her back to him at first. As he felt her strength wane, he spun her around, held her in place, his hand still over her mouth, and looked deep into her terrified eyes. *"I sense your desire to take her. I feel your need. But this one will not be spoiled by you. Tonight, she is only for us,"* Blasphemy said.

"But…"

"Just make it look like an attack. You are to do no more than that," Blasphemy said.

Henry hesitated. Blasphemy took control and forced him to punch her hard enough to knock her out. Gently he brought her to the floor, knelt, and ripped her clothes. He cupped the back of her head, lifted it slightly then with his free hand opened one of her eyelids with his thumb and pointer finger.

In a thin stream of mist, Impa passed from Henry's palm through her eye and into her body. He let go of her eyelid. She convulsed. Using the same two finger to open her mouth, he leaned in and opened his mouth in a gaping maw, extracting her soul as he inhaled. Her essence screamed for help as it left her physical form and was ingested at the same time by Impa.

Henry felt chewing motions within himself as the demons devoured Maya. Her essence nourishment for them. He fell on his side, quivering as his some of his own soul was eaten away. They had been doing that quite often to him on purpose. For with each bite, he felt they made him their slave.

His friend, Drew Beckford, toying with a satanic ritual in an effort to gain power in real estate, had summed four of these demons. Two possessed Drew and the other two chose Henry. Through an unholy pact they agreed to help the demons feed. Henry had more control over them in the beginning, threatening to cut off their food supply if they didn't help him live rent-free and flip apartments. By killing certain residents for his friend who owned rent-stabilized buildings but could not raise the rent on long-standing tenants. Once they were gone, he was given a free place to live while renovating them. The demons did all the work. Leaving no traces of foul play behind. They even aided Henry in his appetite for beautiful women. He attacked; they killed.

But these demons soon realized how much he needed them and had decided to toy with him. They tethered themselves to him, controlling his actions and denying him the women he desperately wanted, leaving him frustrated.

"I know you wanted the woman, but you will have another chance. You need to leave now. Go out the back way. We have had our fill for tonight,"

Blasphemy said. "And stay away from the store. The old man and the cat don't like you and we don't need extra trouble."

Henry slowly rose to his feet and staggered out the back. Moved into a tight alley between the buildings, he made his way to the street and walked one more block to the building where he was staying.

III

The next morning when Louis opened the store Barry was waiting to step out. He meowed. Brushing his head against Louis's leg, he went out onto the sidewalk and looked down the street for Maya. She usually stopped in for a bottled water and a bacon-egg-and-cheese sandwich shortly after opening. He walked in the direction of her apartment and sat in a ray of the sun to wait.

He closed his eyes and sniffed the air, looking for that horrid smell from the night before. There was none. But his hearing picked up the faint sound of police sirens in the distance. He opened his eyes just in time to see two police vehicles turn the corner ahead, continue straight for several feet, then stop. There was movement, people running into a building and then the sirens of an emergency vehicle. It turned the corner and stopped behind the police.

Barry saw a person running toward him. A woman named Angela, whom he had known since he was a kitten. She had a panicked look on her face as she raced past him and into the store. Barry started to follow when he noticed a crowd of people down near the center of the block. His curiosity got the best of him and he sauntered toward the crowd instead, sensing their urgency mixed with panic. He began to jog as other people ran past him. Weaving his way through people's legs, he managed to get to the front of the crowd where the police gathered. They were keeping people back as the EMTs, one male and one female, made their way in with a gurney. Barry slipped unnoticed past everyone and entered the building.

The EMTs were at the far end of the hall under the stairs. A police officer, two men in suits, and a large heavyset man with a ring of keys all stood there looking at something. The police officer guided the heavyset man away as the EMTs disappeared out of sight.

Barry got closer. That's when he smelled his own scent, mixed with several other odors that ranged from sour to salty. The closer he drew he picked up on one more smell. Not as strong as the others, but he recognized it immediately. Henry and his putrid stench. Barry turned and looked under the stairs.

Maya lay just a few feet in front of him, her face badly bruised and her clothes torn. The EMTs stood to the side watching two men in black suits. The one kneeling over Maya had slick black hair and wore glasses. He was examining her face and body. The other stood over him taking notes in a pad. He was slightly older with no hair.

"Coroner is gonna have to figure what killed her. These bruises didn't. And there's no in blood anywhere," the kneeling man said. "What do you think, Detective Summers?"

"Yeah, I have to agree with you," the bald man said. "There's no forced entry at the door. No real sign of a struggle, and no one heard anything." He closed the pad. "Higgins, we gotta catch this guy."

Detective Higgins stood. "There's a connection here. Something about this building."

Instinctively, Barry meowed. All eyes looked in his direction.

"Where did the cat come from?" Detective Summers said.

Barry slinked past everyone, jogging to Maya. Sniffing her, he yowled.

"Oh my God, is that her cat?" Detective Higgins said.

"There are no pets allowed in the building," A voice called out as they approached. "Not sure whose cat that is. We have a lot of strays around here. Probably one of these bodega cats." He looked at the detectives. "My name is Drew Beckford, I'm the owner of the building, how can I help?"

Barry had not seen this human before but he reeked just as bad as Henry. Instincts kicked in. He growled as he backed up and put himself between Drew and Maya. Drew stepped closer and Barry swiped at him and hissed.

"No closer, please," Detective Summers said. "Do you have cameras on the premises?"

As Drew and Detective Summers talked, Detective Higgins turned to Barry and knelt.

"Hey, buddy, it's okay." The man reached out and scratched him under his chin. Barry purred and brushed the man's hand with his head, then went back to protecting Maya's body. Detective Higgins reached for him, but Barry growled. "Interesting."

"Coroner is here," one of the EMTs said.

A young man carrying an evidence sheet stepped up and looked at Barry.

"What's with the animal?"

"He's standing guard," Detective Higgins. "He won't let me move him."

The coroner stepped up and tried to move Barry, but he wouldn't go. He worked around him, certifying she was dead. Only when he opened the evidence sheet did Barry move several inches away. Once it covered Maya, he climbed on top of her and balled up.

"I've seen this before. Animals do grieve you know. He must have really loved her," the coroner said. He turned to the EMTs. "You can take the body."

The EMTs wheeled their gurney over, lifted Maya with Barry on her, and placed her on it. As the headed for the door, Barry hissed at Drew as they glared at one another.

"Poor Barry. That cat loved that girl," an onlooker said.

Drew's eyes grew wide. Barry yowled again. Then he heard voices like the ones from Henry only these entities did not show themselves.

So you're Barry. We have heard about you. The fighter. And as it looks, a protector. Well not so much. As you can see, we still got her. Do yourself a favor and stay out of our way. There are more of us than you. Take this as our final warning. If we meet again, death will befall you.

Barry yowled and laid his head on Maya's body. Detective Higgins followed them out to the street where onlookers talked amongst themselves and pointing to Barry. When the EMTs reached the coroners van, Barry jumped off her and slipped through the crowd.

When Barry cleared the people he looked back at Detective Higgins who was coming down the stairs. The detective made his way through to the edge of crowd and stopped.

"Hey, Barry, c'mere." Detective Higgin knelt and rubbed his fingers together. Barry ran to him. Purring, he let the man rub him. "You know who did this, don't you? You know who we're looking for."

Barry felt the sincerity in the man's voice. He placed his paws on Detective Higgins and stood up on his back legs. Staring into the detective's eyes, he meowed.

"I'm gonna keep an eye on you. I hope I'm around if you see him," Detective Higgins said.

"Higgins!" Summers called. "Let's head out."

"Copy that," Detective Higgins said then looked back at Barry. "Find him for me, Barry."

Barry meowed then jumped down. He glanced Higgins' way before leaving.

IV

Barry had spent most of the day in the stockroom out of sight. The Health Department had been by looking for him and Louis had to hide him. In addition, Louis knew Barry was depressed about Maya like they all were. When the coast was clear, he left the door open for him to come out.

Barry wasn't depressed, he was stressed. He couldn't get the demon's warning out of his head. He had heard of older cats who used to live in the neighborhood doing battle with supernatural elements before. Cats were known to have very close ties to what humans call "the other side." They could sense the dead, and even angels and demons when they were close, although it was easier to feel the good than the bad. Evil wasn't something a cat wanted to get near but if forced to fight and defend against it, they would fight. He needed to find this thing and either force it to flee or destroy it. The feral instincts in him began to brew.

Barry decided to try and find the demons. What he would do when he did, he wasn't sure yet. He stepped out into the bodega and saw Julio standing by the door talking to Louis.

"I can't believe what happened. I had just left her. How could that happen so fast," Julio said.

Barry crept between them and Louis reached down and scratched him behind the ear as he left.

"Be safe out there, Barry," Louis said

He walked past the playgrounds, searched the backyards of brownstones and townhouses, and even the foyers of apartment buildings but came up with nothing. There was no sign of Henry. Barry talked to two other bodega cats but neither of them had come across Henry but promised to report anything if they did. On his way back to Louis, Barry visited a store on Classon Avenue between St. John and Sterling Place, where he saw a group of humans gathered talking. An elderly woman named Alice, who Barry knew well because she always gave him a cat treat when she came by the store, was crying on the shoulders of the store owner, Miguel, who tried to comfort her.

"It's sad, she was such a nice girl," Alice said. "What monster would do such a thing?"

"People been letting their guard down around here," Miguel said. "Neighborhood changes, gets gentrified, and people think crime can't happen around here."

Barry felt their frustration. He calmly approached Alice and brushed against her. He startled her but when she recognized him she knelt and pet him from head to tail. With each pass he felt her calm down and once she had composed herself, Barry continued back to his store.

He made an effort during his walk to comfort every human that called to him, or that he felt was in distress. The more he could help them feel better, the more grief he freed them from, the stronger his self-worth grew. By the time he got back to the store, he felt ready to take on the evil staking a claim in his barrio. The demons weren't going to gain any footing without a fight.

U

Word on the street was Maya had died of a heart attack during the assault, but many did not believe that because of her age and how healthy she was. What really made the neighborhood gossip was how Drew listed her apartment on the market within days, move-in-ready and no longer rent stabilized. By the end of two weeks, a new tenant had moved in.

Drew's reputation for buying and selling real estate around the neighborhood made him both the talk and fear of property owners. If he appeared at someone's door, chances were he was about to make some kind of offer. That was probably Louis' thought when Drew walked in because he wasn't known to frequent the bodegas. He stopped in infrequently to get a water or cigarettes but that was it.

When he entered, he greeted Louis and Julio warmly but kept goose-necking for Barry at the bottom shelves and around the counter.

"You lose something," Julio asked.

"No, I was just looking for… do you guys have a…" Drew spotted him near the Doritos. Barry stalked out and began yowling. "There he is. That's Barry. Henry told me all about him. He's calm now, huh?"

"So you're still here. Your days are numbered cat. My brothers and I will see to it you're disposed of."

"I haven't seen Henry around since Maya's death," Louis said.

"He's been dealing with some property over in Manhattan for me. He should be back by next week though. Can I get a pack of Chesterfields?"

"You don't seem that concerned. Give us a moment."

Louis retrieved the cigarettes. When he placed them on the counter, Drew touched the top of his hand. Louis trembled then passed out.

"Louis!" Julio hurried around the counter to help him.

"Is he okay?" Drew moved around to assist. He glanced back at Barry as he touched Julio's shoulder and he collapsed. "Get him."

Two spectral demons stepped out of Drew's body and solidified. One had a maw of teeth scales and looked blind. The other bore wild red eyes and massive claws. They charged at Barry, forcing him to scurry.

Red-Eyes leapt on him, seized him by the neck and tossed him into the stand filled with potato chips. Barry crashed through the bags, sending them across the floor. He landed on his feet but Scales seized him and tossed him back to Red-Eyes, who slashed at him, nicking him in the neck.

Barry yowled and hissed. He started to rush Red-Eyes but it fled around the shelf of canned goods, putting distance between them. It stopped at the far end and slashed at him. Barry skidded to a stop and turned to retreat but Scales blocked him. Barry tried to jump on the shelf but Scales grabbed him by the tail and brought him down to the floor. It held on and flung him over its shoulder into the front door. Bary struck the glass hard and fell on his side. His legs wobbling, he stood up but fell over.

"Give him one more round so he understands what he's dealing with," Drew said.

Scales rushed to get him. Grabbing Barry by the neck, it lifted him so they were face to face and roared.

Barry cried out and lashed out with his claws, scratching Scale's nose and bottom lip. The demon sizzled as its wounds blistered and smoked. Scales dropped him. Barry turned his attention to Drew and charged. He leapt up into his face screaming and scratching. His claws ripped flesh. Drew immediately backed away from Julio and Louis as Barry positioned himself between them.

Scales moved to Drew and reentered him. *"Move,"* it said and Drew put more distance between them and Barry.

Red-Eyes jumped over the counter on the other side of Louis and suddenly realized it had trapped itself. Barry jumped over the humans, landed on the demon scratching and biting while Red-Eyes backed into a tight corner, screaming in agony as its body smoked and boils formed and popped. Barry seized it by the nape of its neck and dragged it out from the corner. When he let go, it scurried back over the counter and jumped back inside of Drew.

Scales had Julio by the ankle and tried to drag him away. Barry went over the counter and around to cut it off and with one hard swipe, laned all of his claws across its face. It ran to Drew and jumped back inside him.

Hurt, Drew ran for the back door and disappeared.

Mewing, Barry ran to Louis and licked his face. Seconds passed before Louis came to and looked at Barry.

"What happened? Did I pass out?" Louis asked.

Barry meowed and continued to lick him until he sat up. Then Barry turned his attention to Julio and repeated the process. When both men were back on their feet, Barry ran to the back and found the door ajar and his attackers gone.

The brief encounter put Barry on his guard.

During the day, he sat outside the store alongside the ice freezer watching people walk by waiting for Drew or Henry to pass, visibly on guard. At night he made several trips to Maya's building and stayed under park cars watching to see if either would show. He repeated the routine for two weeks but saw neither of them.

A few times at the store, Casey stopped in to complain about Barry coming and going. She and Louis even got into a screaming match after he accused her of calling the Health Department on them. Barry watched her with narrow eyes. When she turned her attention on him, Barry looked away. He had no time for her.

Three weeks after the fight, Barry went on a late patrol of the neighborhood. As he neared Maya's building, the demons' the rancid scent tainted the air. He quickened his pace as he followed it. Fifty feet from the tenement, he spotted Henry coming out of the alley between the buildings, wiping his hands on his shirt and talking to himself. Barry froze and watched him.

"I'm back in control now. You owed me," he said, "Now fix my bruises."

"*We… the cat is here,*" Impa said.

"Get him!" Henry said.

"*Not here. We're not exposing ourselves,*" Blasphemy said. "*I have plans but not tonight. Run away. Do it.*"

Henry's demeanor changed. He appeared frightened. He ran in the opposite direction. Barry started to give chase when he noticed the pungent odor down the alley. He changed directions. Scurrying down the alley, he discovered a young woman face down on the ground, her clothes torn. He trotted to her, sniffing her hair and licking her face. She lay there lifeless. He climbed on her back and loosed loud desperate yowls into the night. His sad cries echoed up to open windows and eventually someone called the police when they looked out and saw him with the victim.

Detectives Higgins and Summers arrived to find Barry standing guard at the mouth of the alley. They acknowledged his presence but said no more about him as they conducted interviews and inspected the body. They discovered two things: she was a resident in Maya's building; and bruising on her knuckles indicated she had fought back. But there were no witnesses to the actual crime. After several hours, once the body was removed and the alley was sealed, the detectives started for their car. Detective Higgins saw Barry again but this time he was facing the building and sitting in a pouncing stance. His tail thrashed like a metronome as he stared at the building.

"Look," Detective Higgins pointed to Barry. "He's in hunting mode."

"What?" Detective Summers said.

"Cat's do that when their waiting to pounce." Detective Higgins looked back at the building. "He's waiting for something or someone."

"We have a lot of paperwork to do. Leave the cat to his business. Probably looking to kill a rat."

Detective Higgins knelt and pet Barry but the cat never took his eyes off the building.

For the next four nights, when Detective Higgins drove by the crime scene on his way into work, he spied Barry patiently waiting. On the fifth, he witnessed something unusual. Barry bristled in defense mode his focus locked on Drew who stood on the steps of the tenement staring right back at Barry. A clear stare-down. When Drew spotted the detective, he went back in the building. Barry lowered his defenses and sat normally. Barry's demeanor convinced Higgins to return to the tenement for a talk with Drew, and to investigate the alley further.

After that night, Drew disappeared. Henry did as well. And for several weeks, tenants of the building moved out, fearing that they would be targeted next. The sudden mass exodus was followed by a blacklisting of the building in the market. No one wanted to move in. Drew's absence was noticed and rumors spread that he had abandoned the property or had plans to sell it.

Barry still made his rounds. He stood watch as tenants moved out, hoping Drew would show his face. But no rancid smells or signs of Drew or Henry surfaced. What did happen one afternoon caught Barry off guard.

Casey moved in. She told Louis that a friend with an inside track on the neighborhood rental market told her the building she had been living in was about to increase its rent. They in turn suggested Drew's building and was able to get her a great price on a larger apartment. She loved the neighborhood too much to move out of it, so she took the offer. She never said who made the offer, but there was some speculation that she must have made a side deal to get the size apartment she did. She bragged that she was not concerned with the attacks because she was always mindful of her surroundings.

No sooner had she moved than she targeted Barry with increased aggression. Especially when seeing Barry patrolling back and forth then going in the store and laying on things. Her complaints to Louis and Julio fell on deaf ears, at first, but when they got a visit from the ASPCA about animal cruelty, Louis banned her from the store.

When the ASPCA didn't take Barry, the Health Department made a surprise visit one evening with Casey in tow. Barry slipped out the back. He circled the block and by the time he was in eyesight of the store, Casey stood outside talking to the Health Department agent. Louis stepped out and the three argued. Barry slipped under a parked car and stayed out of sight until everyone went their separate ways.

Eventually Casey walked past him and headed back to her building. She started to go up the steps but paused, turning to look toward the alley. She said something and Drew stepped out from the darkness. Casey stepped back down and greeted him. They spoke but Barry couldn't make out what they were saying. Carefully, he moved under the parked cars, getting closer to them.

"Bet you've been wondering where I've been, huh? We know you've been watching the building. We decided it was best to lay low until we came up with the best way to deal with you," the demons within Drew said.

Barry watched Casey enter the alley, with Drew following. Barry, low to the ground and focused, slipped from under the car to the mouth of the alley. Listening, he heard nothing. When he peered around the corner he spied nothing at the far end. Their stench, however, permeated the air. He crept into the shadows. He was halfway to the back when two red eyes appeared in the darkness of the adjacent wall. Barry froze. A hand seized him but he immediately scratched at it. Something howled and scurried away. Barry's eyes adjusted to the low light revealing Red-Eyes running down the alley. Barry gave chase.

When he reached the far end, Red-Eyes, a demon with a horse head with horns, and another black, oily humanoid with tentacles for hands waited for him. That one pointed to him.

"Grab him!" Blasphemy said.

Red-Eyes moved first. Barry turned to defend himself. Scales, whom he didn't see, came from above. Landing atop of Barry, he pinned his body against the ground. Red-Eyes moved in next and palmed Barry's head. Impa, the horse demon, glided across to Barry, leaned close to his eyes and smiled.

"Eyes are the gateway to the soul, Barry. Say goodbye to yours." Impa turned into a thin mist and entered him through his eye.

Barry felt it slide in, like a needle pulling thread through skin to stitch a wound closed. As the demons let him go, he screamed and writhed, clawing first at the air, then at his body as the foul presence snaked through him, feeling like the top of a scalpel, pricking and scraping inner flesh. His lungs started to be compressed, like full balloon being mashed and the air forced out. He started hacking like he had a hairball but he couldn't expel Impa. A type of gaseous bubble formed in his gut, expanded, and exploded, sending an intense burning through his entire body. In various points inside, he felt Impa hooking its claws into him. Breathing in air was like sipping through a closed straw. His heart raced until his head swam and he fell to his side. He could feel Impa's weight holding him down. Blasphemy moved to the far end of the alley where Henry restrained Casey. His hand over her mouth as she struggled to break free.

"You were right about her hatred for Barry. This worked to our advantage. She is yours," Blasphemy said.

"I need your help, remember. The guilt."

"Fine. Impa can feed in the meantime." Blasphemy entered Henry and they dragged Casey into the building.

Back in the store, during the attack, Scales had dived into Drew to make him move. Barry's eyes narrowed at the memory. Cocking his head, he locked his gaze on Red-Eyes, standing with its back to him. Fighting Impa's control, Barry stalked silently toward the demon. Claws extended, he swiped and scratched Red-Eyes down its back. Snarling, it turned and struck at Barry, nicking him in the cheek.

The side of Barry's face burned like dry ice on flesh and he felt Impa's control lessen. Barry attacked again, goading Red-Eyes to lash back. With each strike Impa's claws snapped loose from his flesh, its weight lifted as the bloating receded.

"Stop that," Impa said. *"You're damaging the host!"*

With satisfaction, Barry felt its panic. Before Impa could intervene, he moved in and bit Red-Eyes on the arm. It hollered and scratched Barry deep across the neck. Seering pain surged through his body as the damage force Impa back to his head and out through his eyes. It solidified from its mist form and attacked Red-Eyes.

"Why are you attacking me?"

"You attacked me inside him," Red-Eyes said in a gravelly tone.

"You idiot, I'm not a tether. I cannot use the host to attack, only feed."

While they bickered, Barry slashed at them both. They fell to the ground writhing as he attacked, their bodies smoking and boiling. When their thrashing weakened, he turned to hunt Scales.

Across the alley, the demon ran toward Drew. Barry raced to beat him there. Using the wall as a launch pad, he flew at Drew's face again. Clinging to the man's shirt, Barry lashed with one paw, reopening the wounds. Drew screamed and stumbled, falling to the ground. Scales missed Drew, landing on the pavement. Barry pounced, wildly slashed up its back before running back inside the building.

In the entranceway, Henry hunched over Casey as she struggled against him. He ripped at her shirt and pinned her hands over her head.

Barry leapt onto his back and sank his claws into Henry's flesh. Letting go of Casey, Henry scrambled to his feet. He tried desperately to reach back but couldn't get hold of Barry. He turned and ran back out into the alley, falling into trash cans. Barry pushed off. Crouched, he stalked around the demon-ridden man until he could see Henry's face then attacked. Henry fell back into the garbage as Blasphemy left his body and lashed at Barry with its tentacle hands.

Yowling, Barry clawed back then darted out of Blasphemy's reach. He scurried close enough to snag a tentacle with his claw then bit down. Blasphemy roared and thrashed as his appendage sizzled.

"*Stupid cat! I'll kill you!*" Blasphemy said. Its tentacle lashed out. Grabbing Barry, it squeezed.

Barry's high-pitched caterwauling drew people to their windows. He whapped at the tentacle slashing with his claws, forcing Blasphemy to let him go. The demon turned to retreat inside Henry. Casey ran past it, grabbed a garbage can lid, and smashed Henry over the head over and over. Blasphemy paused, then turned the other way.

"*Get up, you fools. We need to go,*" he snarled at Red-eyes and Impa, who still sprawled across the alley. "*These hosts are weak and damaged. Do not reenter them.*"

"Fire! Fire! Help!" Casey screamed as she continued to strike Henry.

Barry looked from Casey to Blasphemy and chose to go after the demon. He pounced, clawing at its back. Blasphemy turned quickly and seized him in its tentacles.

"*You did well, Barry. We are leaving. We will not return so long as you leave us be.*"

Barry smacked the tentacle for good measure leaving a long, ragged scratch. Blasphemy let him go, grabbed Impa and Red-Eyes, and fled the alley, disappearing before he reached the end. Scale screeched at Barry then climbed up the side of building and faded away into the night.

Drew sat up and screamed after the demons.

"No! Don't go. Please! I promise to fill the building again. Bring you more souls to feed on."

Yowling, Barry stalked over to Drew and smacked him rapid-fire with his paw. Drew cringed. Barry sniffed him then scratched him hard, ripping his cheek and making it bleed. As Drew fell over gripping the wound, Barry sauntered over to Casey who had knocked Herny out cold.

She sat on the ground out of breath and just stared at him. "Never yell rape, I was told. Yell fire. People respond to fire," she said.

"Hello! NYPD! Who's back here?"

Recognizing Detective Higgins' voice, Barry yowled.

The detective turned the corner with Detective Summers and two NYPD officers following behind. "I'll be damned."

Meowing, Barry ran to him. Detective Higgins knelt down and petted him, then Barry led him toward Casey.

"You okay, miss?"

"This guy tried to rape me," Casey said as she broke into tears. "Barry saved me."

"Good boy, Barry," Detective Higgins said as he gave him scritches. "I knew you knew something was up."

"Demons! Demons made me do it. We were possessed," Drew cried out as Detective Summers and the NYPD officers lifted him to his feet and put him in handcuffs. "The cat knows. The cat saw them."

"He sure did, let's go, pal," Detective Summers said, shaking his head as he looked over to the officers. "He's all yours, boys."

Barry walked to Detective Summers. Rubbing against his leg, Barry meowed then sauntered down the alley. His battered head lifted high, Barry sniffed the air and gave a satisfied sigh. It was clean. He headed back to the bodega tired and beat up.

VI

Barry woke the next morning to the sound of several neighborhood children coming into the store to get sandwiches for school. He had gone back to his spot among the chips where his fans gave him random pets and talked sweet to him on their way out as the store came to life.

After the children left, he climbed out of his spot and sat in the center of the store. Julio came in with news of Henry's capture and the two men went back and forth on how they couldn't believe he had been the store. In the middle of the conversation, Casey walked in. Both men stopped speaking and stared at her.

"May I come in?" she asked.

"Yes… yes, please," Louis said.

She gave them a sheepish smile then walked to the back refrigerator where she took out a container of milk. Quietly she went to the counter and put it down.

"We heard," Louis said. "Are you… I mean… how are you…?"

"I'm okay," she said softly. "I'll be okay." She looked back at Julio. "I'm fine."

"Hey, listen, if you need anything. Anything at all just let us know," Julio said.

"There is something," she said as she put her money on the counter. "Can you promise me something?"

"Sure, what is it?" Louis asked.

Casey turned and looked at Barry. He stared back at her. She slowly knelt and put her hand out. It trembled slightly. Glancing at her fingers, Barry meowed and trotted over to her. She scooped him up in her arms and held him tight, tears streaming down her face.

"Never *ever* get rid of this cat," she said.

Barry licked her cheek and purred. In that moment, he knew his neighborhood was safe.

For now.

Hobbs

DUCKBOB: REUNION
Aaron Rosenberg

Mary is giving me that look. You know the one. The "Have you been concussed recently, is this a many-years-delayed side effect of your transmogrification, or is this in the nature of fourth-dimensional chess and would make sense only if I could see through time and space and possibly transduce both?"

I can't be the only one to ever get that look from a significant other, though admittedly I may be the first to ever have it be potentially true for any of those options. Or to have someone who could probably handle any of those without breaking a sweat.

Anyway, my lovely lady has her head cocked to the side, surveying me and the item I'm carrying. Which is good because, with my bill, it's not like I can see it.

"DuckBob, you are certain this is an appropriate offering for such an occasion?" she asks. Mary's as Earth-born as I am, and as American, but she was always a bit of an odd duck growing up—must be why we get along so well!—and being taken and modded by the Grays didn't exactly help her fit in any better. Quintupled her IQ, maxed out her photographic memory, all that, but may've quashed all those pesky social norms and cultural literacy references in the process.

Fortunately, me? I still got all those. I may not use the former too much—hey, when you're sporting feathers and a duck head you're allowed to act weird, or at least it's expected!—but I got 'em. Which is why I grin at her now and heft my armful. "You betcha. Trust me."

She favors me with a warm smile at that—warm enough that I'm afraid this stuff's gonna melt, and me along with it!—and rings the bell.

Somewhere inside, I hear a tune play off that. "MacCavity" from *Cats*. Nice, and very on-brand.

The door opens, and I have to peer down over my own bill and my delivery to see the person standing there, since it's not like she's gotten any taller. "Hey, Lila."

For a second, my little sister just stares at me, and I feel that spasm between my eyes as I try to look at the same spot she's seeing — mainly to see if there's a little glowy red dot there. Did I misjudge? I thought we were good after the whole "saving the universe together" thing. Was I wrong? Are we back to uneasy silences? Or, worse, her hating my guts?

Then she smiles. "Hey, big brother. Hi, Mary. Happy July Fourth. Come on in." And she steps back, pushing the door open as she does.

Whew.

I follow her, careful with my feet — I can't see what I'm doing and they're the size of tennis rackets so I've got great balance but need to be careful about stepping on things. Or people. Or small European sportscars. She leads us down a hallway and through a living room to a huge screened-in back porch, all bright and airy and festooned with red, white, and blue streamers to denote the holiday. The hostess herself is wearing a "Free since 1776" button, her one sartorial nod to the occasion. "You can set that there."

I lower my arms, trusting her, and sure enough my offering lands on a long table between a Jell-o mold and a Watergate salad. The perfect place for a cheese tray the size of a baseball diamond. "Nice," Lila says, studying it. "Thanks."

"Sure thing." I stretch a little, getting feeling back in my arms — hey, that smoked Gouda weighs a ton! — and glance around, nodding at the other relatives already here. "Nice place, looks good." It's the first time I've seen it, since Lila cut me off while we were both still in college and bought this place a few years later, and I'm thrilled the ban's finally been lifted. I start to say more... but stop as I feel something wind its way around my ankles. Something small and furry.

Damn it, I thought I left the sentient slippers at home!

Lila smiles, though, and reaches down to scoop up... a cat. An orange tabby, to be precise. She drapes it over her shoulders like a stripey headrest, and I can hear its rumbling purr from here.

"Sorry about that," my little sister says. "This is Jake."

"No worries. Hiya, Jake." I hold out my hand, carefully — the problem with being covered in feathers is some critters figure you're their next meal — and Jake eyes it a second before leaning forward and headbutting my fingers. I scritch him and his eyes half-close in delight. Yeah, bud, I'm the same way.

Lila's studying me. "I didn't know you liked cats." She doesn't say it like an insult, though. More wondering. That'll take some getting used to.

"Oh, sure. Me and cats, we understand each other."

Her smile's wider now, and not mean but... taunting? Plotting? Like she's setting me up for something? I've sure seen *that* look before! "In that case, come with me."

I follow her back into the house proper — Mary starts to go with us but then Ma calls out to her and, being a good girlfriend, she takes the heat and goes to greet Ma on our behalf — and across the living room to its far side, where a short hall branches into two bedrooms with a bathroom in between. Lila grins at me as she stops by the second bedroom, opens the door —

— and reveals an entire Kingdom of Cats beyond.

"What the — ?" I try for a quick headcount but keep losing my place because the room's occupants aren't exactly sitting still. No, they're climbing, leaping, tussling, sliding, dodging, all in and around and through what looks like a fuzzy jungle gym that fills the place wall to wall. "Lila, how many cats've you got?"

She shrugs. "A dozen, maybe? They're not really mine." She gestures toward the far wall, and I see a flap's been added below the window there. "I put out food and water and any cats that want to come in can." She reaches over the baby gate I hadn't even noticed across the door and scritches a calico, which stops and purrs before batting at her and flouncing off. "I just didn't want any of them to go hungry or be stuck out in the cold."

That's Lila for you. Comes across mean as a rattlesnake — and can be, if messed with — but she'll do anything for her own. I'm just happy I'm at least edging my way back into that group.

I squat down, poking my fingers through the gate and wiggling them. Two cats wander over to investigate, and both lick my fingertips. "Hey there, fellas."

"You really *are* good with cats," Lila says. "I'd worried that — " She waves a hand at my head, my feathers, all of me. One thing about her not speaking to me since shortly before my abduction is she escaped Ma's whole "don't ever acknowledge what happened to Robert" edict, and I'm kinda glad about that. Not that Lila would've obeyed anyway.

Even Ma could never get her to do something she didn't already agree with or at least didn't care enough to argue about.

"Yeah, it was touch and go at first," I admit, straightening as the cats wander off. "There was this whole thing, though. Happened pretty early on, too." She's got that "let's hear it" look, so I tell her. It feels good to share stuff with her again.

Besides, I remember it all like it was yesterday, crystal clear in my head. 'Course, that could be the fault of those nanite chips Ned fed me — if by "fed me" I mean "brought over to install in the Core's security systems but I saw the bag saying 'chips' and decided they were a snack." I should've realized when I saw they were "RAM" flavored. They were hella crunchy, though.

I'm twenty-three, I look like a duck, I'm plastered outta my gourd, and I'm butt naked.

Also, I'm being chased by the local dog-catcher.

Either he figures I'm his ticket to fame and fortune or he's drunk too and thinks I'm a full-blown hallucination. Though if that's the case, I'm not sure how well he expects to do with that net.

Anyway, I'm charging through people's backyards, leaping fences, tearing through bushes — which hurt, by the way, feathers ain't exactly plate mail! — and dodging sprinklers, swing sets, trampolines, patio furniture, you name it. Normally I'm a klutz and a half but right now the combo of adrenaline and booze are making me a master at parkour.

What trips me up?

A cat.

One minute I've got a comfortable lead, at least two good lunges ahead. The next there's this furry black-and-white blotch tangled up with my ankles and I'm sprawling like a metroplex with an unlimited construction budget and no urban planning.

Wham! I hit the ground hard. Through the ringing, I hear something screeching at and partially under me. Oh, right. The cat. Apparently it couldn't get clear in time.

Next thing I know, there's a net on me. Not all of me, the only people with ones that big are those trawlers you see along the coast, scooping up whole salmon runs at a time. But this one manages to bag one of my feet — impressive in its own right — which means it's got me anchored nice and tight.

And the cat's caught right there with me. It keeps flailing about, trying to tear its way clear. Fortunately duck flippers are pretty tough, but I still feel every scratch.

I glare up at the dog-catcher, a big, beefy guy whose face is now as red as his ears got when I asked him which way to the petting zoo. He smirks down at me.

"Not so funny now, huh?"

No, I have to admit it's really not. Especially since I'm starting to come down from all that booze.

He apparently called reinforcements — and that must've been a fun call, all "No, seriously, this duck's big as a fridge!" on the one side and "Uh huh, pull the other one" on the other — because a bunch more Animal Control types show up. Between them they manage to drag me to my feet and use those pull-chain dog collars as makeshift manacles to hobble and handcuff me. They even work an oversized muzzle over my bill.

Talk about embarrassing. I'm just glad most of the neighbors don't know about my recent life change, so they can't tell it's me just by looking. Even if they guess my identity based on sheer stupidity.

Mr. Dog-Catcher bustles me off to his van and shoves me into this bear-sized cage in the back. Not sure what he thought he'd put in that thing, out here on Long Island. There're smaller cages alongside, but they're all empty.

All but the one housing a sullen, glaring black-and-white occupant with one bent ear.

Sorry, cat.

The door slams shut and a minute later I hear the van start up. Then there's a lurch and off we go.

Great. I've spent a night in jail plenty of times. In the pound, though?

That's a new one.

We pull into someplace and soon Mack the Net is hauling me back out, down a dim hallway, and into a big room lined with cages on either side. Most're empty but a few have dogs, cats, even a possum.

"Hey!" I tell him as he shoves me forward. "Come on, enough's enough. I'm sorry, okay. I've been having a rough time of it. But this, this is inhumane. Literally."

Unfortunately, he's still got the muzzle on me, so all that comes out are a lot of muffled grunts and groans.

He unlocks the biggest cage, right at the end, and body-checks me into it, then removes my restraints and, finally, the muzzle. I grimace, work the kinks outta my bill, and try again.

"Look, I'm sorry," I tell him. "But this ain't right. I don't belong here."

"No?" Mr. Dog-catcher eyes me up and down, but not like he's only now realizing I'm a regular guy under all this fancy plumage. No, more like he's suddenly seeing me as the goose that laid the golden eggs. "Maybe you're right."

He walks off, whistling to himself, and I sink down onto the floor. There isn't even a bench, let alone a toilet—just a blanket at the far end and a bowl of water in the front.

This place is getting a negative Yelp review when I finally make it to a computer.

Something yowls at me, and I glare at the cage across the way. It's that same cat.

"This is all your fault," I tell it. "I'd'a been home-free if you hadn't tripped me."

The way it glares at me, yellow eyes narrowed, I get the feeling it's thinking the same about me.

I sigh. "I don't suppose you've got a deck of cards?"

Pretty sure that hiss was a "hell, no."

I gotta say, sitting there in the pound, naked except for my feathers and the dark cloud over my head, may've been the lowest point in my life. I was still getting used to the whole "turned into a duck" thing—hence getting so plastered I thought it'd be smart to take a late-night swim in the Sound, starkers—and having all sorta existential quandaries about "Am I even a real person anymore?" and "What does it mean to be human?" and "Why do you drive on a parkway but park on a driveway?" Being scooped up like a stray wasn't exactly helping. So when Mr. Dog-catcher returns a little while later, I barely look up. Until he laughs.

"Guess this's my lucky day," he says. "Turns out there's some kinda agency that's real interested in strange stuff. Little green men, flying saucers... guys who look like Daffy Duck, only real. Got a couple'a them coming by first thing, and they've promised me a big fat finder's fee." He grins at me. "So, yeah, thanks for getting me all riled up. Never would've chased you down otherwise." He whistles to himself as he turns and saunters back out.

Great. Now I've got some wacky government types coming to collect me at dawn. I can guess what that means, I've watched enough cheesy movies. I'm about to spend the rest of my life being poked, prodded, dissected, experimented on, turned into a murderous cyborg, grown to ten stories tall, you name it.

I gotta get outta here before that happens.

Only problem is, how? I get to my feet — that bare concrete was murder on my joints! — and really inspect my cell for the first time.

And once I do, I smile.

Like I said, I've been in jail plenty — all of us in the family have. They've actually got our name on the wall of one cell, though that's mainly because Frank and Jimmy smuggled a marker in with 'em one time. Anyway, I know jail cells.

This? This thing is meant for dogs, cats, bears, runaway ostriches. It's big, sure.

But it was never expected to hold somebody with opposable thumbs or a C- in Shop class.

I tug experimentally on the door. Yeah, there's give to it. Another tug. Still more give. Okay, hold that thought. I back up a pace or two, do my best Van Damme, and give it a solid kick right on the doorplate. Hey, I'm no Bloodsport champ but when your feet are the size of a motorcycle sidecar they pack plenty of punch, training or not.

The door flies open.

Yes!

I step out into the hall, breathing the sweet air of freedom. Okay, it smells like a bunch of unhappy, unwashed animals, but it's the thought that counts.

As I'm about to walk away, something yowls at me.

It's the cat. The same one that got me into this mess.

Then again, it could say the same about me. And probably just did.

I squat down by its cage and we eye each other, fowl to feline. "Yeah, I hear you," I tell it. "And you're right, we're equally to blame. So, no hard feelings?"

And I pop open its cage. The darn things aren't even locked. Why bother, when you can't unlatch it except from the outside?

The cat eyes me a second before creeping forward. I don't move and it edges a bit farther, setting one paw out of the cage, then another. A second later it's free, too — and rubs up against my knee.

"Yeah, you're welcome. Come on, let's get the hell outta here."

'Course, having freed one, I can't exactly leave the rest, right? That wouldn't be fair. So as we make for the exit, I open all the other cages, too. Most of the captives burst out the second I do. One or two stay huddled inside. The possum plays dead. Well, whatever. I gave 'em the opening, up to them to take it.

My new buddy, though, stays right at my side the whole way. She — pretty sure — keeps winding around my ankles, but at least she isn't trying to trip me up anymore.

We're almost to the door when we hear somebody approaching it on the far side.

Crap.

I dart to the side just as the door opens and Mr. Dog-catcher enters. He stops just inside, though, staring at the animals milling about loose in front of him. "What the — ?"

No time to be subtle so I give him the bum's rush, slamming my shoulder into his chest and sending him flying back. Thanks for the football lessons, Ma! Doesn't hurt, either, that my new best bud did the whole "bind your ankles" cat trick at the same time. We make one helluva team. "Let's go, gang!" I holler, leaping over the guy and almost flattening him with my feet as I race out, all my freed friends charging along behind me.

We make it outside a minute later and the animals all scatter. All except the cat.

"You gonna be okay?" I ask her, crouching down again. She headbutts my bill and purrs. "Well, all right then. Take care."

When I straighten up and head for home, she doesn't follow. But I can feel her watching me go.

"And ever since, cats and I get along great," I finish, reaching out to scritch Jake again.

Lila laughs, shaking her head. "Only you could get picked up by the pound. Must've made for an interesting after-report."

"Yeah, no kidding." I frown. "Funny thing is, I wonder if that's what first put me on the MiB's radar? They sure knew where to find me, all those years later." 'Course, if they hadn't, I'd never have wound up at the Galactic Core, never have met Mary or Tall or Ned, never have become the Guardian of the Matrix. My whole life would be different.

Guess I owe that cat a whole lot more'n I thought.

I'm still pondering that when I notice my little sis frowning, though not at me. "What's up?"

She shakes her head. "I don't see Mia. And she never misses lunch." Her frown deepens. "I don't see Ringo or Aster either. That's not right."

"You think they got nabbed?" If they're strays, or even just outdoor cats, there's a good chance. Animal Control's always been a bit overzealous out here on Long Island. I think it's 'cause most of them're probably failed cops and catching somebody's pet's the closest they can get to "making the big arrest." Lord knows we used to mess with 'em enough when we were kids. I'm just glad old Mr. Thurston retired while I was in college — if it'd been him who caught me that time, he'd have spayed me outta pure spite.

Lila's got her serious thinking face on. "Maybe. But most are too smart to get caught by the idiots around here." She shakes her head. "I'm worried it's something worse."

I don't like to see my little sister upset, and I'm thrilled it ain't at me this time, so I don't even hesitate. "Then let's go find out."

She cocks her head at me. "Yeah?" No mention of the party she's currently throwing, with at least a third of our family already here and the rest probably soon to descend like a wave of locusts (which isn't far off when you see what they do to a spread) but that's Lila for you.

"Absolutely." I offer her my arm, and she actually cracks a smile as she takes it. "Let's go check on your cat crowd. Family'll keep."

Funny thing is, they will, too. We've never been big on ceremony. Most of 'em will understand when we get back and explain why we left, especially if we make it back before the fireworks. Oh, sure, Eddie will be miffed, but whatever. Lizzie will just be annoyed we didn't invite her along. The rest, they'll just nod and say, "Sure, cats needed you, we were all good here, no worries. Though you're out of beer."

I might owe Mary for leaving her with Ma for an extended period, however. That could cost me.

We're halfway through the front door when someone small and blonde latches onto my waist. Should'a known I'd never escape unnoticed.

"Hey, Uncle Bob! Where're you two going? Can I come?" Lizzie beams up at me, knowing full well I can't say no to her. Believe me, I've tried. I even tried in different languages, just in case, but *no va*. She's as much my Kryptonite in Spanish, Japanese, and Welsh as she is in English. Fortunately, she rarely takes full advantage of that, which is another reason she's my favorite.

"Some of your aunt's cats are missing," I tell her now, giving her a quick squeeze. "We're gonna see if we can find 'em. And of course you can."

"Great!" Lizzie releases my side — which is good, because maneuvering both of us through the doorway was gonna be tough, I have enough trouble with just me! — and bounces past me and outside. Show-off. I'm still working out the spatial geometry to clear the frame — regular doors were not made for a man-sized duckbill! — when a hand lands on my arm. Gently but with all the pull of a tractor beam.

"Is there an outing of some sort?" If the touch hadn't already told me who it was, the dulcet tones and razor-sharp enunciation would've done the trick.

I smile up at Mary — yeah, she's taller than me, so what? "Yep, some of Lila's cats're missing. We're gonna see if we can find 'em."

My lady love nods. Then she hip-checks me — and I slide through the doorway like a greased pig. Yeah, she's way better at spatial stuff than me, you should see her at multi-phase pool. Her quantum bank shots are the stuff of legend. "Excellent," she declares, following me out and shutting the door firmly behind her. "Where shall we start?"

I glance over at Lila, who shrugs. "I leave food out by the park," she says. "Most times a new cat shows up, they followed me home from there." She heads off in that direction. I only vaguely know this area, since she cleverly moved to a different part of Long Island, close enough for family gatherings but just far enough to avoid too many uninvited visits. Plus in a different legal jurisdiction, which never hurts. Especially with my family. She doesn't seem bothered by our little fact-finding expedition having doubled in size, which is cool. Though I do notice she grabbed her messenger bag on the way out. I have no doubt it's stuffed full of her trademark pink baseballs, which she fires off like a petite, grim-faced cannon.

Me? I'm happy. It's a nice day out, heading toward a pleasant evening, and I'm walking around with some of my favorite people in the world. Okay, actually my top three — Tall's off-world with Heidi on another interstellar trucking run so I don't have to worry about offending him, even in my head. Yeah, I'm fully capable of having someone mad at me only in my thoughts. Guess those teachers who said I lived in my own little world weren't far off, they just didn't realize I'd populate it quite so thoroughly.

The town's not much different from where we grew up, which isn't surprising. For some reason, our whole extended clan has stayed close by. All except me, of course. Can't get much farther than the center of the galaxy! Hell, just the fact my apartment's in Manhattan weirds most of 'em out. Anyway, it's pleasant out here, with wide sidewalks, nice little houses with pretty front lawns, and one-way streets in decent enough shape. The park's fair-sized, not Central Park by any stretch but maybe Madison Park-sized and a whole lot more open, just a wide swath of green with paths cutting across north-south and east-west, trees here and there, and a nice-sized gazebo where they intersect. I can see a playground just past, and tennis courts, but here there's nothing but greenery and the occasional bench. There's nobody else about, and it's real peaceful.

Too peaceful.

"Where're the birds?" I ask. My three companions — my family — stop and glance at me. "No, seriously." I wave my hands around. "No birds?"

Because it *is* quiet. Too quiet. A place like this should have a ton of birds in the trees, insects buzzing about, squirrels, rabbits, you name it. A good park's teeming with life.

I have the feeling if I were to dig my foot in the dirt anywhere around here, I wouldn't even find an earthworm.

Lila nods. "You're right. It's never this quiet. Something's wrong."

Mary turns in a slow circle, and I have to remind myself I'm with my niece and my sister so I shouldn't stare. "I am detecting anomalous energy particles," she states. "Non-terrestrial in origin." She gestures past the gazebo, and now I see what I thought was maybe light from a lamp post or something, except if I squint I can tell it's going straight up into the sky.

Oh, you gotta be kidding me. Lila's cats aren't just missing, they're being abducted? What're the odds?

Well, at least we've got the experts here. Both Mary and I've been through this ourselves.

"Okay, time to put a kibosh on the *kit*napping," I declare, shoving up my sleeves—which is unimpressive both because they're short sleeves anyway and because my arms would make a twisty straw look muscular—and stomping toward the gazebo. I can see the light through it, and march clear across the tidy little structure, leaping out the other side—

—and almost getting sucked into the energy beam there myself.

"Whoa!" I flail my arms, catching myself just in time—this bill's got a lot of momentum to it, when I'm old I'm gonna have the reverse of the usual "hunched double" posture 'cause I'll have spent so many years bending backward I'll be shaped like one of those little staples you use to hold cables in place. I manage to stop myself, regain my balance, straighten—

—and find myself staring a cat in the face. It's a big, fluffy gray, and it looks just as surprised as me, its blue eyes wide as it drifts up past my head.

"Aster!" That's Lila, who throws herself clean through the beam, scooping the cat up as she does. She lands cleanly on the other side—I think she and Lizzie got all the grace in our family—snuggling the cat to her.

Lizzie and Mary're next to me now, one on either side, and we all stare at the energy beam. "Where's it going to?" I ask, peering up. "I don't see anything there."

Mary got different alterations from the Grays, including the ability to see into a whole bunch more spectrums. She tells me I'm lovely in ultraviolet. Anyway, now she nods. "The origin point has been shielded." Raising her arm, she taps something onto her watch. You think you've got a smartwatch? Next to hers, yours is like an untrained puppy, all yips and licks and fumbled responses to repeated commands.

A second later, a ship appears right over our heads.

My first thought is, "Huh. Haven't seen that model before."

Okay, so maybe I'm pretty inured to the sight of alien ships. Happens when you've shuttled around the galaxy a time or three, fended off multiple incursions, yadda yadda. Anyway, this one I don't recognize. It's small, sleek, and iridescent, but there's something about it, some feeling at the back of my head. It reminds me of something else. I just can't figure out what.

"Whoa. Neat." That's Lizzie. I forget that she and Lila and the rest've only just learned about my real job or where I actually live. They've seen a handful of things, way more than most, but it's all still new enough to be surprising. Which, I gotta admit, must be pretty cool.

"Very nice," Lila agrees, her tone indicating anything but. She's circled the beam to rejoin us, Aster still in her arms. "But why's it stealing my cats?"

Mary frowns, still studying the ship. "I am not sure. The design—it is Phelinorian. They are an insular race. I would not have expected to find them this far from home, nor engaged in such activities, for they are nonhostile, desiring only to be left alone."

I nod, but my eyes are still on the ship—and the small speck that just slipped from it into the beam. A speck that's rapidly approaching us, getting bigger as it does. "Let's ask 'em."

We watch as it descends. By the time it's head height it's as wide around as me, which means it barely fits in the beam—I'm a little offended by that, not gonna lie—and I can't help staring. We all do.

Because what we're facing—is a cat.

Not just a cat, though. Because it's sitting on top of a second critter, this one wide and round with stubby tentacles below and big bright eyes and short pastel fur.

It's like somebody crossed a My Little Pony with an Anime octopus. Totally adorable, but I've seen enough "aw, isn't it cute—why's it trying to kill me?" aliens not to fall for that.

Lizzie, on the other hand, is already making "Aww, can I have one?" gasps next to me.

"Okay, you in charge here?" I demand, doing my best to glare at the thing. Which isn't easy, especially when I realize it's got a dopey little grin under those eyes. "We want our cats back!"

Mary nods. "That is a Phelinorian," she confirms. "I am uncertain why it is serving as a conveyance, however."

"Because it wants to. And we like it."

That answer doesn't come from the cute fuzzy thing we were expecting to respond, though.

It comes from the cat.

Not that the cat spoke—that'd be silly. But I hear the words in my head, and from their reactions I can see the others do, too. And there's no doubt who sent them.

"So you're okay?" I ask the cat. "You're not being taken against your will or anything?" I have a quick mental image of cats being herded into a big bag labeled "snax" and hear the mental equivalent of a purr in response. Yeah, I project a lot. Least, that's what one therapist told me, though I doubt this is what she meant.

"We go of our own free will," the cat answers, and there's a funny little undercurrent of pride and stubbornness to that, like "How could it ever be otherwise?" Okay, fair enough. There's a reason "herding cats" is an expression.

"Mia, you want to go?" Lila asks. I know her well enough to hear the tiniest wobble to that, and to know what she's really asking:

"You want to leave *me*?"

The cat purrs at her, and leans forward out of the beam to headbutt her shoulder. "You are kind," it tells her. "We appreciate you. But they offer us a whole world, and lives of comfort and companionship. How could we resist?"

Lila nods. She holds Aster out to look the big gray in the face. "You want to go too?"

Aster purrs in response. Even I understand that one.

My little sister would never force someone to stick around. She offers Aster up to the other cat, Mia, and a second later both of them are perched atop the Phelinorian.

"Thank you, sharp-edged human." It's a different voice than before, and I figure it's gotta be Aster's. "Perhaps we can still visit you for treats and pets?"

Lila smiles, though her eyes look suspiciously damp. "Any time. You know where I am, door's always open."

Both cats blink slowly at her, and their combined purr's loud enough to compete with a decent lawn mower. "We will visit, then," they promise.

Lila turns away—I know it's so nobody can see her cry—but the cats and their new friend don't go yet. Instead, the one she called Mia focuses on me. And I look at her. Really look.

She's a good-sized cat, with black-and-white blotches all over. I get the impression she's no spring chicken, though she still looks strong and healthy.

And one of her ears is bent.

"No way," I whisper, taking a half-step forward. "You?"

"Hello, bird-man," Mia tells me. "We meet again."

Lizzie and Mary're both looking at me and I know I'll have to tell the story again later. "Yeah. I had no idea you knew Lila."

"Your littermate is kind," she answers. "As are you. Thank you for freeing me, all those years ago. And for coming to free me now, though I did not require it." She smirks at me—cats're good at that. "If not for you, we might never have known beings such as these could exist, nor thought to seek them out."

"Uh, yeah. You're welcome." I rub the back of my neck. "Nice to see you again, too. Take care, and don't forget to write."

She purrs at me, clearly amused. The Phelinorian blinks, and then they start to rise, all three of them. A second later, they've disappeared into their ship and it fades from view, the beam winking out as it does. After staring at that for so long, it's like we're plunged into shadow, even though it's still light out.

Lila punches me in the arm. "So you gave Mia the idea to find aliens of her own? Thanks a lot, big brother." She's not really angry at me, though. If she was, I wouldn't be able to use that limb anymore.

So I just shrug. "Sorry. Wasn't planned. But hey, they seem happy. And they'll still come see you. Maybe you'll even get to go with 'em some time."

Mary nods. "No outsider has ever been allowed onto Phelinor," she says. "That would be a great honor, and would bring much new knowledge to the universe."

I can see Lila's considering that. "Huh. Yeah, maybe." We turn back toward her house. Birds and insects and such're starting to creep back into the area, so it's feeling a whole lot less eerie. "At least they're okay."

We're walking up her front path when Lila turns to me. "This kind of thing happen to you a lot?"

I laugh. "Like you wouldn't believe."

She nods and favors me with a little half-smirk. "Guess it's good you're back, then. Should make life more interesting."

I hug her quick, before she can fight me off, and let go while I still have all my motor functions. "You too, sis. You too."

Together, we all head back inside. It's almost dark, there's plenty of food, and later there'll be fireworks. Plus my little sister's house is about to become a waystation for every cat traveling to and from another planet.

Yeah, I'd say that feels about right for an Independence Day.

I wonder if they're gonna need a whole planetload of cat toys? I'll have to mention that to Tall when he gets back, maybe he and Heidi can nab the shipping gig. I'd say he'd never believe how it came about, but he knows me too well.

Want more DuckBob? Check out the first novel about him, No Small Bills!

![Tuppence 2015-2025]

SOCIALIZATION

One of the greatest impediments to adoption for cats is a disinterest or even fear of humans. Whether the animal has been abused, abandoned, or simply born wild, instinct will tell them avoidance is the key to survival.

Socialization is the method used by cat rescues to improve a feral cat's potential for adoption, as opposed to being released back into the wild. It can be a long process, depending on the cat's disposition, previous treatment, and their level of exposure to and acceptance of humans. To be clear, socialization is not the same thing as domestication. All cats, regardless of their situation, are domesticated. Socialization specifically refers to how well a cat is acclimated to human interaction.

For cats born in the wild — what we typically think of as feral — that is their home. They are comfortable there and can fend for themselves. They do not welcome the presence or intervention of humans and have no interest in a life inside a human home.

For former pets that find themselves in the wild — what are termed strays — they may or may not wish to reestablish a connection to humans, depending on their experiences and how long they have been in the wild. Some of them may have run away, others might have been abandoned, but the longer they go without positive human interaction, the more likely they will become feral, as would any other domesticated animal if human influence is removed.

The younger a feral is the more likely it will be possible to socialize them so that they are adoptable, particularly if they are rescued as kittens. With strays, resocialization is wholly dependent on how soon they are rescued and how positive their previous interaction with humans was.

The process of socialization is carefully, patiently acclimating the cat to the presence of humans, their spaces, sounds, smells, and touch. This can be as simple as being in the room with them, petting them, talking to them gently while taking care of them. It is often a long, slow process and requires an attentive person able to read the indicators revealing the cat's level of comfort and working with it. Socialization is as much about proximity as it is about actual touch. The more comfortable a cat is with humans, the more likely they are to be placed in a home.

Karma, one of our interns. She and her siblings were rescued from beside a busy intersection during the pandemic. Here she is being socialized.

A HARMLESS, NECESSARY CAT
Nancy Jane Moore

THE AFTERNOON SUN POURING THROUGH THE WINDOW MADE A SPOTLIGHT on the bed. Sam lay in the dead center of the light, sprawled on his back, his large white stomach soaking up the rays.

Jean Bowers glared at him from the doorway. "There you are, you naughty boy," she said.

Sam opened one eye, looked at her, shifted his position slightly, and then closed it.

"Right in the middle of Anne Wilson's bed, and you know she doesn't like cats."

Yawning widely, he rolled over so that his back faced the door, lifted a hind leg, and began to lick it. Lazily.

Jean scooped him up. He mewed a protest in the soft, high-pitched tone that always surprised people, coming as it did from a seventeen-pound cat. "I hope she doesn't find out you were in here. She already disapproves of you being in the house. Anyway, you're late for your afternoon appointment with Miss Emily."

Once in Miss Emily's bedroom, Sam became businesslike. He jumped down from Jean's arms, strolled over to the bed, and leapt up on it, landing lightly so as not to jostle the frail woman lying there.

"Hello, Sam," she said, wiggling her fingers just a little to call him closer. He had already begun to purr loudly. Walking up to her fingers, he sniffed, then pushed his head against them. Satisfied, he moved in a little closer so she could rub his head without reaching.

While Sam and Miss Emily engaged in the mutually satisfying ritual of cat petting, Jean unlocked the cabinet in the corner of the room. She took out two bottles and disposable syringes. "How are you feeling this afternoon, Miss Emily?" she asked in her professional nurse's voice as she filled one of the syringes.

"Better than yesterday. I'm sure it's all due to this rascal," Emily Wilson said, scratching Sam's ears. "Look at him, so dignified in his black tuxedo and white spats." Sam nuzzled her hand, and Emily gave him her full attention as Jean stuck the needle into her arm. Her eyes closed briefly—marks up and down her withered arm showed how many injections she'd had in the last few months—but she didn't flinch away, just held the cat close.

Jean disposed of the used needle in the sharps container and picked up the second one. "How's your pain level—if you're feeling better perhaps you want less morphine today."

"It'd be nice not to feel so doped up," the patient said. "Why not? I feel like living dangerously." She laughed a little.

"I'll give you a half-dose," Jean said. "If things change, you be sure and buzz me, and I'll give you the rest."

"You just leave this boy here, and I'll be fine."

Jean left her patient in Sam's care and went downstairs to fix herself a cup of tea. Incorporating "cat therapy" into her work as a home-care nurse had been a stroke of genius. Though she'd had to fight for it with the agency. Sure they'd read all the studies about how animals could help the quality of life for seriously ill persons, but for a live-in nurse to bring a cat with her! She'd had to find her first patients on her own, but their glowing references had made the difference.

Of course, it wasn't appropriate in all cases. There were always those odd people who really didn't like cats. But for others—and especially those dying from painful cancer like Emily Wilson—the cat was a source of comfort.

Anne Wilson came into the kitchen while Jean's tea was steeping. While she couldn't have been any older than Jean's own thirty-five, she affected the manners of a much older woman. It probably helped in her work—she had taken family leave from her managerial job at a large engineering firm to take care of her mother.

"Ms. Bowers," she said, "Your cat has been in my room again. I would appreciate it if you would make a better effort to control him."

"I'm very sorry," Jean said. "I guess I didn't close the door to my room tightly enough, and he got out. I'll try to be more careful."

"Please," said Anne Wilson in a tone that sounded more like an order than a polite request. "I am highly allergic."

Jean looked at her. The woman's eyes did look a little red. Perhaps she did suffer from cat allergies.

"Where is the animal now?"

"With your mother."

"Shouldn't you be there with them? My stepmother" — she emphasized the prefix — "is too weak to make him go away if he starts to bother her."

"I'm sure she'll be fine," Jean said, but the woman's eyes bored into her. She hurriedly tossed out the tea bag, though the tea was only about half-steeped, and went back up to the sickroom. Where she found both patient and cat comfortably asleep.

Though Anne Wilson was annoyed by the cat's presence, Miss Emily's only other close relative was firmly in agreement that Sam was a valuable part of her care. Mark Gibson was Emily Watson's nephew, and though he didn't live in the house, he came by daily, sometimes for several hours, despite his position at one of the city's major law firms. If Anne had come to stay with her dying stepmother out of a sense of duty, Mark made it clear that he spent time with her out of love. He handled her business affairs, and let everyone know he did it free of charge.

"She practically raised me," he told Jean one evening after supper. They were eating ice cream — Anne had left the table, muttering about the evils of dairy fat. "I'd never have been able to afford law school if Aunt Emily hadn't helped me out." He swallowed the last of his ice cream and then put the bowl on the floor. "Here, kitty, kitty, kitty."

Jean looked up. Sure enough, Sam was in the room. He'd gotten her door open again — thank goodness Anne was gone. He walked over to the ice cream bowl and started to lick before Jean realized what he was doing. "Mark, please, take that away from him."

"But I put it down for him." the man objected.

Jean had reached the bowl by that time and picked it up herself. "It's not good for him," she said, apologetically. "The vet keeps lecturing me about making sure he loses a pound or two."

"You're not fat, are you boy," Mark said, picking Sam up. "You're just a big guy, that's all." He set the cat on his lap, and Sam promptly jumped off. He sniffed around where the ice cream bowl had been, and finding it gone, gave Jean a dirty look and stalked out of the room.

"Sorry," Jean said. "Sometimes I think cats are like that line in one of Dorothy Parker's poems — 'I loved them until they loved me.'"

Mark said. "There must be something I can do to make friends with him."

"Well," Jean said. "He does like catnip. And that won't put any weight on him."

"I'll try it. Maybe you can help me make Aunt Emily see reason, too."

"Why, what's the problem?"

"She insists on continuing to manage her financial affairs. And of course, with her money, they create quite a lot of work. I've tried to get her to sign a power of attorney, let me deal with her stock broker and so forth, but she won't do it. Insists I bring the papers over to her and let her make the decisions. I know it exhausts her."

"Some people have a lot of trouble letting go," Jean said. "But it might be helping her fight the cancer, knowing that she has responsibilities, decisions to make. She's doing better these last few days. I'm sure it's hard on you, being the go-between..."

Mark interrupted. "No, no. I don't mind that. It gives me more time with her. I just hate tiring her out."

Jean found herself thinking about Mark a lot. A handsome man, with the dark hair and blue eyes that always caught her attention. And he flirted in that friendly way she'd always found appealing.

The way that always ended up breaking her heart, she reminded herself firmly. Besides, he was younger than she—and all the young women in town chased after him anyway.

Several days later, after she and Sam had given Emily her bedtime medicine—she seemed to be doing fine on less morphine—Jean met Anne just outside the bathroom they shared.

"Ms. Bowers, I'm afraid I'm going to have to talk to the agency about your cat."

"But your mother is doing so much better since he came. She needs less morphine, gets more rest."

"It's all in her head. And I'm reduced to taking antihistamines just to get some sleep." She held a package of twelve-hour capsules in her hand. "I'll call them tomorrow."

Jean tossed and turned, trying to get to sleep. She didn't want to have to leave this post. It would look bad on her record to be asked to leave because of Sam. And even though she'd get other jobs, she hated the thought of taking him away from Miss Emily. He'd brightened up her days, given her a little joy. Why her daughter—all right, stepdaughter—should be so unwilling to see that, Jean couldn't imagine. Surely she could get shots for her allergies for the short period of time Emily had left.

Sam didn't sleep well either. Every time Jean turned over, he'd get up and move. It seemed like hours before they both finally drifted off.

Jean woke suddenly. It seemed as if she'd only been asleep a few minutes, but the alarm clock read 3:07. A streak of light shone into her room—the door stood ajar, letting in light from the hall.

She heard a noise—loud scratching sounds and an even louder "meow." Sam must be trapped somewhere, probably the closet. She jumped up, opened the closet door. But it hadn't been completely shut, and no cat ran out.

Putting on her robe, she went out into the hall. The yells and scratches were coming from Emily's room. How had that cat gotten her door open, and Emily's, and was then shut in? It made no sense.

Jean opened the door to Emily's room, and Sam shot by her. She saw him race into her own room. I'll just check on Miss Emily, she thought, opening the door a little wider. She didn't want to wake the woman.

The room seemed quiet. Too quiet. Emily usually snored a little. In the dim light, Jean could see that her hand hung limply over the side of the bed.

Her professional manner took charge. She turned on the bedside light to get a better look. Emily's wig—she'd hated the hair loss from chemotherapy and insisted on sleeping in it—was completely askew. And her eyes stared at something with blank horror. Jean reached for her carotid artery, to check the pulse, and leaned forward. But she already knew Emily was dead. And not from the cancer.

Jean turned to the phone and dialed 911. As she explained to the dispatcher who she was and what had happened, Sam came cautiously around the door. He jumped up on the bed and tried to nuzzle Emily's hand. "Mew," he said. His tone sounded sad to Jean.

The police had arrived by the time she'd been able to wake Anne up. And it had taken her a while to locate Mark. She'd only gotten the answering machine when she called him at home, so she'd tried his cell phone. From the sounds she heard when he answered, he was partying somewhere.

Now they were all downstairs, waiting for the medical examiner to finish his preliminary exam. Anne was sitting in a corner chair, sniffling. Jean wondered if it was allergies or grief. Mark was pacing around the room. The glass of bourbon in his hand sloshed dangerously as he paced.

Two police officers waited with them. The one in charge—a balding man in his late forties—was drinking a cup of tea. The other, a young woman, leaned against a wall. The forensic team had already left.

The medical examiner came in, carrying something in a large plastic bag. The detective in charge looked at him expectantly. "Suffocated," the examiner said. "I found a lot of cat hair around her face, and..."

"I knew it," Anne said loudly. "That damned cat, sleeping on her face."

"He wouldn't do that," Jean said, shocked.

"That terrible animal," Anne said, but the medical examiner cut her off.

"It wasn't the cat, ma'am. Though it looks like someone tried to hold him over her face—I found some cat hair in her mouth. I'll know more after the lab work, but it looks like the cat struggled to get away. Something ripped a hole in a pillowcase; I found a piece of cat claw in it."

He held up the bag. "Whoever killed her used this pillow." He looked around the room.

The chief detective cleared his throat. "So, Ms. Wilson, you said that only you and Ms. Bowers were sleeping in the house tonight."

Anne nodded. She seemed unable to speak.

Jean said, "Mrs. Wilson didn't care for live-in servants. Someone came in daily, to clean and do some cooking."

"Did any of the help have keys to the house?"

Anne shook her head.

"Did anyone else who wasn't here have one?"

Jean felt rather surprised that Mark didn't speak up. She said, "Mr. Gibson has one, of course. No one else that I know of."

"I was at a party all night," Mark said hastily. "And I must point out that while my aunt thought very highly of Jean," —he nodded toward her— "she did come here from an agency, and we don't really know anything about her. You hear these terrible stories, nurses killing their patients."

Jean was so taken aback by this accusation that she could think of nothing to say.

The medical examiner cleared his throat. "A nurse wouldn't need a pillow," he said. "Had she wanted to kill Mrs. Wilson, she could easily have used the morphine prescribed for her pain. Much harder to detect."

The chief detective said, "We'll check out everyone's bona fides. But unlike you and Ms. Wilson, Ms. Bowers didn't stand to inherit a lot money when Mrs. Wilson died."

Both Mark and Anne stared at him.

"She was dying anyway," Mark said. "Even if either of us could be so cold-blooded..." He let his voice trail off.

"I loved her," Anne said. "Kill her for money? I loved her." She broke down totally, sobbing. "She helped me so much. Showed me what a strong-willed woman could do in this world." She made great gulping noises. "It hurt me so, to see her in such pain. I couldn't stand it."

The woman detective handed her a tissue. Anne blew her nose loudly, and repeated, "I couldn't stand it."

Jean saw the detective raise her eyebrows at the one in charge. He nodded. Like her they were probably thinking mercy killing. But mercy for whom? Miss Emily hadn't seemed ready to die to her.

And then the medical examiner said, "What's that cat doing?"

Sam, who had been nuzzling Mark's leg for some time, was lying on his back, rolling around, and purring loudly.

Jean said, "He must have found some catnip — that's how he responds. Mark, did you get him some?"

Mark said, "No," loudly. A little too loudly. Sam grabbed around Mark's leg with both forepaws and nuzzled the sharply-creased cuff on his pants. Mark tried to shake him lose, and something fell from the cuff. Sam pounced on it, and Jean pounced on him. A couple of leaves lay on the floor.

Sam meowed in protest. The medical examiner bent and picked it up. "Is this catnip?" he asked Jean.

She nodded. "Fresh-picked."

"I found leaves just like it on Mrs. Wilson's bed," he said.

"I don't have any, but I did tell Mark he could use it to make friends with Sam."

Everyone in the room turned and looked at Mark. He said, "You don't think I did anything? Why that's preposterous. I would never harm Aunt Emily."

"How'd you get that scratch on your hand?" the woman detective asked.

"I don't know — I did some drinking tonight. Could have happened anytime."

"Looks like a cat scratch to me," said the medical examiner. He started walking toward Mark. Mark moved away, but the examiner turned instead to the cat in Jean's arms. "Let's see if there's anything on your claws, pussycat."

And Mark ran for the front door. He moved fast, but the chief detective moved faster. "I think you'd better come downtown with us, Mr. Gibson."

Jean had expected to have to return for the trial, but once they'd run all the DNA tests, Mark plead guilty. She got a brief letter from the detective.

"Unfortunately, the motive was the most obvious one: money. Gibson had embezzled some money from a client and was close to getting caught. The loan sharks had told him they wouldn't lend him any against his expectations from his aunt until she died. He was in too deep to wait a few months.

"The enclosed is for Sam. He made this one easy for us."

The enclosed turned out to be a small version of a detective's gold shield, attached to a cat collar. Sam protested a bit when Jean put the collar on, but when she walked him over to the mirror to admire it, he batted at the reflection of the shield. And purred.

Spot

NINE-TENTHS OF THE LAW
Christopher J. Burke

OFFICER SQUILLON WASN'T THE LAZIEST MEMBER OF THE SMALLPORT CITY Guard. He just tended toward creative solutions that involved some procrastinating. And he didn't really hate his job, especially not in the daylight hours. But he found walking the dark streets from lamp to lamp and from shadow to shadow to be trying at best. He just wanted to make it to the end of his shift in one piece. And he wanted to maybe make one collar along the way to keep the Sarge off his back.

That's why on this night Squillon included a stop at the Drop-Dead Goblin on Basilisk Road, the rowdier of the two taverns on the south side. Anybody who spent their day lifting a hammer, shovel, broom, or axe was welcome to lift a pint. Dockworkers and shopkeepers, lamplighters, and street sweepers, anyone with a thirst and a coin would crowd inside its walls.

Squillon had a pouch full of coins and a bit of a thirst, so he'd go where the drunk-and-disorderlies gathered. Nabbing a couple meant returning to the station for a couple quiet hours of scratching quill against parchment. Of course, the side perk of drinking on duty while waiting for an inevitable brawl to break out never failed to lift his spirits either.

The tower clock struck twelve. Many considered it the witching hour. Squillon considered that ridiculous. For one thing, wizards in Smallport conducted their business any time they pleased. For another, magic took a physical toll, and most mages liked their beauty sleep.

No, he thought, *midnight only announced that the second day of the month has begun.* And he knew that a lot of grunts and scuts had gotten paid on the first when the sun had set. So there'd be an abundance of sullen and surly wretches packing the Goblin, drowning their miseries and blowing off steam.

This caused Squillon to smile as he made his way up Market Street. He took his time, stopping to check locks on shops and peer down alleys, until he reached Basilisk Road. Then Squillon stopped for one final check. He straightened his vest and adjusted the collar of his official navy-blue cloak, with copper trim denoting his rank. Then he checked that his baton and short sword were secured. When he was done, he stepped around the corner. Lively music greeted him, but it was drowned out by shouting before he plodded another twenty paces.

It's going to be a good night, he thought.

In no time, he figured, the fists would be flying, either in spite of or because of his presence. One good scrum, and he'd spend the rest of his shift at a desk, feet up, with a hot mug in hand.

I should be so lucky, he thought. *A bust like that on my record, I could coast for days!*

It was unfortunate for Squillon that Lady Fortune led him astray.

The copper had just reached the entrance to the Goblin when he heard a disturbance in the side alley. One hand on his baton, Squillon retrieved an illumination coin from his vest pocket with his other. Retail spellware wasn't cheap, but it beat carrying a lantern. Once uncovered, the coin lit up most of the narrow lane like the first rays of dawn. He saw something move in the shadows. A pair of green irises, low to the ground, peered out from behind the bins.

Is that an animal or a human, he wondered. *Or gods help me, something in between?*

In-between creatures were not unheard of in Smallport, but usually only seen and spoken of by those who had a few too many drops of the creature themselves.

Squillon stopped at the alley's entrance, and shouted, "You there! I can see you! Come on out!"

The officer didn't know if whatever was there understood the Common tongue or not. Either way, he could make out movement as it backed up and rose into the light. Then he choked out a disgusted grunt, and briefly turned his head. "Sir, why are you naked?"

When the man didn't respond, Squillon had no choice but to approach. He observed no obvious injuries. Maybe this was a bad prank taken too far. On the other hand, something worse might have occurred. If this man was a victim of a crime, the officer would have to bring him to the station to take a statement. Then the whole thing could be turned over to the detectives in the morning.

"Sir, do you require assistance?"

Of the responses he might've expected, the loud hiss he heard was not among them. The copper stopped for a moment at the sound, but then inched a few steps closer.

In response, the unidentified male crouched low to the ground. Without warning, he sprang for the dust bins. Squillon assumed that he meant to leap onto or over them. But some miscalculation caused the naked man to crash into them instead. The officer stood and watched as the guy toppled to the ground, covered in trash.

The suspect rolled away. He jumped to the back wall of the alley. Despite clawing and scratching, he couldn't find any purchase, and slumped back to the floor.

"Definitely not drunk." Squillon considered other possibilities, including bewitchment or possession, and all the dangers that went with them. He let go of his baton, and pulled out his cuffs. "I don't know what's wrong with you, fella, but we'll figure it out at the station."

The suspect was wiry, but the alley was narrow. He had no chance to slip by. The officer watched the guy pace back and forth just out of his reach. He seemed to be assessing his surroundings while never letting his attention drop from Squillon. Whenever the copper inched forward, the scrawny fellow spit at him.

Despite the man's erratic behavior, Squillon managed to move in and cuff one wrist. This immediately brought the subject under control. When the other side snapped close, the enchanted cuffs glowed and hummed for a moment. Mages had said that these cuffs could tame a bear. No one had ever tested that theory, but completing the circuit did render regular people docile. However, it didn't make him any more cooperative. The man stayed silent and stared off into the night sky above. Plus, he was still as naked as the day he was born.

Squillon waved the light around. "Where are your clothes?"

Instead of waiting for an answer, he walked over to the tavern's back entrance. With a shove, the door opened into the kitchen.

"Wait there." Squillon stepped inside, and returned a minute later with a tablecloth. The guy hadn't attempted to run away. In fact, he was in the same exact spot, but sitting on his legs, and licking his hands. The officer looked up to see if the moon was full.

Squillon covered the subject as best as he could, and then marched him down the street. The two made their way along Basilisk Road without any struggle, turning down Broad Street, toward the south side precinct house. It was one of the few free-standing buildings in the area, and the only one with a carriage house behind it. On any given day, this area bustled with activity. But after dark, a skeleton crew ran the operation.

When the pair walked into the station, Sgt. Grisler, the Desk Officer, looked over the new arrivals. "What do we have here? And what the hells is he wearing?"

The confrontation didn't affect the guy's disposition at all. He didn't seem to be aware that they were talking about him.

"Public indecency. And possible charm, possession, or other bewitchment."

"The station wards should cancel most charms and spells." Grisler looked back down at his paperwork. "Take him downstairs and put him in the tank. Let him sleep it off. If need be, we can run him over to Downtown in the morning. Let them figure out what kind of crazy he is."

Squillon led his guy down into the cellar. The creaking of each step under their feet did nothing to wake up Brodsky, asleep at his desk. It was a slow night, and the cages stood empty. Squillon hit the desk with his baton. Brodsky jumped.

"Catch forty winks?"

"Hadn't even gotten twenty yet." The napper composed himself, and then looked the prisoner over. "What's his deal?"

"Don't know yet. We're holding him until morning."

Brodsky led the unknown man to a cell. Squillon removed the enchanted cuffs. Immediately, the man grew agitated again.

He tried to push past the two officers, but was easily rebuffed. When the door had slammed shut, he pressed his face between the bars, as if trying to squeeze through. Bored with that, he turned his attention to his surroundings. Finally, he sat on the cot and curled his knees to his chest.

Through all of it, he didn't utter a single word. Not in Common, nor any regional tongue or dialect.

Squillon sighed. He sat for a moment on the edge of the desk. "The sarge was right about one thing. Getting a doctor, priest, or wizard in the middle of the night ain't an easy thing to do. Not if it isn't a dire emergency. And we don't even know which one we need! With luck, that guy just needs a cot and a blanket until whatever misbrewed concoction he drank wears off. And a pair of pants!"

Brodsky laughed. "I can't do anything about the pants, but he's good until morning."

On the bright side, Squillon realized he'd gotten what he'd been angling for. The paperwork would keep him off the street for at least an hour. Two if he pushed it. Naturally, the report would have gaps in it. The suspect's identity was unknown. He had no tattoos that might give a clue to where he hailed from or what he did for a living. He had a scar running down his chest, possibly an old knife wound. Talk about bad luck. Knife attacks happened often enough that even if it had been reported, it would be impossible to find the records without specifics. Since such a search would take more hours than he had left on his shift, he signed the parchment just to be done with it. At that point, he allowed himself to sit back and enjoy a moment of tranquility.

The dark cloud to Squillon's silver lining was that he now had to go back out on patrol. He almost didn't mind it though. By this point, most of the riffraff would've left the streets, having gone home of their own volition. Nothing left to do but rouse some vagrants.

Without anything else to detain him, the copper started back out. That's when he heard Sgt. Grisler holler, "Bullfinch! Why the hells is that woman wearing your cloak?"

Another officer had walked into the station, out of uniform. He was accompanied by a barefoot, red-headed female. She had a familiar absent-minded look. The woman wasn't part of the Guard, and definitely shouldn't have been wearing a Guard's cloak. But Squillon suspected the reason before Bullfinch answered.

"She's naked, Sarge. I found her like that just walking the streets. But not, you know, walking the streets."

Grisler's head snapped in Squillon's direction. Their eyes locked, except that the sergeant's were silently screaming. He didn't need to be clairvoyant to read his thoughts.

Bullfinch looked back and forth at the two of them. "What?"

The sergeant turned back to Bullfinch. "You, take her downstairs. And you, go with them. See if those two recognize each other. Maybe you'll get some answers."

"Who two?"

"I'll fill you in on the way down. Let's go."

In the cellar, they swapped a blanket for Bullfinch's cloak. He hung it on a hook, not eager to put it back on. Squillon glanced at the protective glyphs sewn into the cloak. They'd proved as ineffective at altering the woman's behavior when she'd worn it as the wards had been when she entered the building.

Brodsky was leery about putting both people in the same cell, but he complied with the orders from the man upstairs. The guy appeared to be sleeping. But as soon as the door slammed shut, his head craned around. He was up and alert. And his blanket fell to the floor. Squillon sighed and walked away.

The two cellmates backed to opposite sides, and then started circling. At no point did they exchange words. They just locked wary eyes on each other.

"Do you think that 'Red' and, uh, 'Fred' know each other?" Bullfinch asked.

"No idea. But they don't seem to trust each other. We should probably sep—"

Before he could complete that thought, Red launched herself at Fred.

"Brodsky, open the door! Now!"

It took a few minutes, but calm was restored. The possessed pair had been separated with only minor amounts of scratches on all the parties involved. The three officers watched the other two pussyfoot about their cages, where they alternated between watching and ignoring the other. Finally, both hopped onto their cots.

When they were satisfied that things had settled down, Squillon and Bullfinch returned upstairs. Reports needed to be written and amended. And with morning approaching, arrangements for transportation must be made.

For once, Squillon found himself wishing that he'd stayed out on the beat. He could've spent his shift patrolling quiet cul-de-sacs, looking for that ever-elusive band of thieving kobolds. But even as dawn drew close, this strange night wasn't done with either him or the south side precinct just yet.

Sgt. Grisler started yelling again.

"What do you mean, 'They're gone'? Where the hells could they go?"

Brodsky stood petrified. His mouth hung open. He held up his ring of keys so tightly that his knuckles had turned white.

The only thing that could possibly make the situation worse was the voice that asked, "Where did who go?"

All eyes turned upon the front door. Captain Millstone had arrived early, as he was wont to do. He was the no-nonsense head of the precinct. Those under his command found him to be quite affable when you got your job done, but rather surly when you screwed up. He was accompanied by Detective Sergeant Potch, who didn't start her shift for another hour. That they showed up together was likely a coincidence and nobody's business.

The pair looked around at everyone, waiting for a reply.

"I repeat, where did who go?" There was no doubt that he expected an answer.

Sgt. Grisler finally spoke up. "Officers Squillon and Bullfinch each brought in possibly possessed individuals, whom they found wandering outside, naked, and—"

"What? *Again*?" Det. Sgt. Potch interrupted.

The captain turned to his detective. "And what do you mean by 'again'?"

She removed her cloak, which notably had silver trim instead of copper, and folded it over her arm. "There was an incident a month ago, over near Bakers Row. A seamstress came in. She said she'd woken up in the middle of the night, and saw a naked woman sitting in the gutter, just staring out into the night. She took the woman inside her boarding house. But in the morning, the woman was gone. No one else was missing. Nothing had been stolen. Detective Lurren and I canvassed the area, but no one had seen anything. She just vanished. That is, if she ever existed in the first place. We wrote it up as unsubstantiated."

Millstone nodded. "That actually rings a bell. I want to see you and Lurren when she gets in. Twice in two months isn't a coincidence. It's a pattern. Squillon, Bullfinch, my office, now."

The "yes, sirs" were interrupted by a frenzied call of "Captain Millstone!"

The bedraggled appearance of the man who burst into the station belied his actual position.

"Sir Kistle? What the devils…?"

The nobleman had obviously dressed in haste, without the help of his servants. Squillon noted the way the man fought to catch his breath and guessed he run all the way and hadn't waited for his carriage.

The desk sergeant brought some water, and Kistle guzzled quickly.

"You need to take all the men you have to my house at once!"

"Sir, please. Maybe you would like to step into my office, and talk privately."

Capt. Millstone reached out to take the gentleman's arm, but Kistle pulled away. "I don't need to be coddled. I need you to go arrest my housemaid!"

Every officer in the room exchanged silent glances, but none dared speak. It was solely the captain's place to question a person of Sir Kistle's station.

"Sir, we are eager to serve, but I will need some more information. Why is it necessary to send all the men and women under my command to your house to arrest your maid?"

"Because she's a witch!"

A different kind of crazy, Squillon thought. But noble crazy couldn't be taken Downtown. Not unless you wanted to spend the rest of your career mucking out stables.

"I knew she was one! I had a suspicion about her! She disappeared one night last month, and acted like nothing had happened. All the doors remained bolted, yet she'd gone and somehow returned. Then last night, I confronted her! And — and —"

He withdrew a little and started to adjust his attire. He'd become aware of his disheveled appearance.

"And?" Capt. Millstone prodded.

"And she turned me into a housecat! Suddenly, I'm on all fours on the floor with gray and black arms. And paws!"

Kistle surveyed all the faces looking at his. "Don't look at me like that! I tell you, she turned me into a tabby and then chased me about the room. When I managed to climb atop the china cabinet out of her reach, she turned into a big, black cat herself. Bigger than I was. And she leapt up beside me.

"I jumped off and fled, but she chased me around the entire house! The entire house!"

The room remained quiet for a moment. Bullfinch and Squillon looked at each other. Brodsky took a special interest in his key ring. Grisler stared down at his desk.

"It wore off as the sun rose. I dressed myself and hurried here as fast as I could run."

That part of the rambling account piqued Squillon's interest, and another crazy thought occurred to him about how the prisoners escaped. But he wasn't free at the moment to voice it, so he held his tongue. *Still,* he thought, *if Sir Kistle actually did turn into a tabby, and his maid, as well, wouldn't the reverse be possible?*

Capt. Millstone spoke politely, giving the story the respect that matched its teller's status, whether or not he thought it true. "Okay, sir. Trust me when I say that we will take care of this."

The captain turned to his officers, and spoke in a more measured tone than they might have expected. "Detective Sergeant Potch, take these two officers, and escort Sir Kistle back to his house. Talk to the servants. I'll send Detective Lurren along as soon as she arrives. Send the officers back at that point.

"Sergeant Grisler, send a page to summon the wizard-on-call. Now. I have a theory, and I need some answers."

When the captain approached Brodsky, who still clutched his keys, the officer broke down. "I wasn't sleeping, sir. I swear."

Millstone ignored his pleading. "Go back downstairs, and look for a pair of cats. Check in and under everything. Use a broom if you need to, but get them out of my station."

Puzzled, but without questioning the order, Brodsky disappeared into the cellar. The sound of the squeaking steps faded in the distance.

Squillon grabbed his cloak. He stopped to ask, "About the cats, sir."

"You have a theory, Squillon?" Millstone withheld a smile. "Let's hear it."

He took a deep breath and hoped it wouldn't sound ridiculous when spoken out loud. "Some magics, particularly when conducted by poorly-trained practitioners, can have unintended side effects. I might surmise that a side effect of turning a particular person into a cat might be…" He paused and swallowed. Squillon surveyed Millstone's face, looking for any reaction, before continuing, "might be… turning a cat… into a person."

To the officer's surprise, the captain nodded in agreement. "Yes, that's my thinking as well, which is why I sent for the wizard-on-call. I think you two managed to wrangle a couple of feral felines last night. And when the both of you get back, you'll spend the day sweeping out the cellar. Everyone in this station knows I'm allergic to cats!"

Officers Squillon and Bullfinch nodded. Both knew better than to bring up clocking out in another hour. And pulling one double shift was better than a month of them. They just hoped they were getting paid for it. Not that they would bring that up, either.

FOSTERING KITTENS
Amber Davis

"How did you get involved in fostering kittens?" is my most commonly asked question! I am happy to answer!

I'm a busy mom, I work as an artist full-time from home, part-time job outside the home, and occasionally do art shows on weekends. I wouldn't say I have a bunch of "free time" but my husband, myself, and my children have a lot of love to give and the knowledge to help kittens, as we have been cat owners all our lives. That doesn't mean there have not been challenges along the way.

I personally didn't really know about the fostering process and never really knew who to ask, but in January 2016, a friend of a friend posted on Facebook, looking for a foster for two kittens or they would be "put out" as they were found alone outside in the mean streets of Philadelphia. She said all food, litter, and vetting would be provided, and even a dog crate to house them in; I just needed to help them grow big enough for adoption, to be fixed, and socialize them as they were a little spicy. That was *so* tough as they turned out to be very sweet kittens, and then I kept getting asked to take more in after my last batches left and then; like a revolving door, I found myself fostering for a local non-profit cat rescue in Philadelphia, who focused on abandoned, stray, and abused cats and kittens. After a few years of fostering for two different rescues and becoming a champion of finding forever homes for needy kittens, I ceased fostering after the passing of close family members in 2020, needing the rooms for other family to move into my home. I also had two foster fails during all these litters of kittens; Ludo, an orange tabby, (DOB Oct 2016) who attached quickly to my newborn son, and Moxy (DOB March 2017) who, a bit shy, attached to me.

After moving to South New Jersey in 2021, I realized I was about a ten-minute drive from the animal shelter in this county, and I found myself with the extra space I needed to house needy kittens. After prepping a designated space in my basement with some drywall, insulation, and floor tiles (for easy mopping) I just picked it right back up with South Jersey Regional Animal Shelter, about ten minutes from my house.

Fostering had its challenges at first, being introduced with administering medicine and fluids to sick kittens. This was a learning curve, on what all the illnesses were, and how they affected myself, and other kittens in the household (and even my own resident cats.) While fostering a mom and five kittens in my sunroom, the kittens excitedly surrounded me ready to be fed. Accidentally, I stepped on a kitten's paw, to which the mother cat reacted to attacking me viciously, and relentlessly to a point I was screaming for help and my husband had to come and pry her off my face. New glasses, rabies shorts, and many scars later, I found myself more careful around any mothers with kittens.

I attached to one of her oddball kittens who was the runt and seemed to be delayed in everything, and was suspected to have "swimmers' syndrome" in which their legs splay out, instead of being under her body when walking. Some YouTube videos and a little bit of hands-on help, we helped her get past that phase rather quickly and she grew by leaps and bounds. After weeks and weeks of relentless begging, my husband finally agreed to let us keep this little kitten, Izzy, who we suspect is a rare genetic natural mutation of a Devon Rex breed cat. She has an odd wavy coat, wiry tail, and a kink at the end of it, she had since I get her as a neonate kitten.

Next few litters or groups were good, until they weren't and my kittens kept getting sick one after another. There is nothing more dreadful than going to check on your kittens to find one has died. My heart broke to pieces when this happened for the first time, and unfortunately it was not the last. Paluk is a vicious viral killer in young kittens who are born to unvaccinated mother cats, and it is extremely contagious, deadly, and can live on surfaces up to two full years if not cleaned properly.

After losing one after another after another, my heart could take no more and I took a break to re-evaluate my set up and my sanitizing methods. I found that keeping kittens and mothers in an open space like a room (and a carpeted room, for that matter) was not the best way to foster groups after groups. After about a year, I acquired three different

enclosures to keep in my basement kitten space to keep all kittens separate from one another. Doing this, and disinfecting everything properly has dramatically reduced the deaths of kittens.

Fostering ANY animal, for as short as a time as a weekend could literally save that animal's life and help them decompress from the hectic, noisy shelter and help them blossom into the pet they can be! No time is too short. No life is "too busy." Make time to help those who cannot help themselves.

Learning from your mistakes and learning from your foster kitten peers is the best way to grow and learn as a foster mom. It is absolutely heart wrenching to lose kittens. Feeling their life fade from their body as they take their final breaths in your hands is absolutely devastating... but spaying and neutering and vaccinating your cats would prevent this needless suffering. I will continue to foster and advocate for those who don't have a voice until I no longer can.

Amber Davis
Vineland, NJ

HOARDER
Bernie Mojzes

It had been over a week since Machka first discovered this remote farmhouse. He'd walked for weeks across the barren landscape, across blighted fields and through blasted forests, scrounging food where he could find it, and water whenever a pond or creek didn't stink too badly of corruption. There was a town, a few days' walk back, where he'd hoped to find refuge. Most of the buildings were still standing, there, and inhabited, but the townspeople were hostile. He'd barely escaped with his life.

So he moved on, and found this.

The farmer was no friendlier than the townspeople, chasing Machka off with a shotgun. Still, the farmer could only be in one place at a time, and as long as Machka was careful of both the man and his traps, he could sneak into the granary at night and get enough food to sustain himself.

These days, Machka called that a win.

During the daylight hours, Machka hid, nestled safely beneath dried brambles within the copse of dead trees that bordered the field.

It hadn't always been this way. Once, the world had teemed with life. Machka remembered fields of green, broad-leafed trees full of life — songbirds and squirrels and chipmunks that danced among the branches — all gone now. The change had come slowly at first — long stretches of unbearably hot days, brutal storms and sudden floods — and then all at once.

Once upon a time, Machka lived in a house. Now the house was gone, washed away, along with his family, leaving only mud and flies.

Others suffered a different fate, and Machka had walked through fields of ash up to his chest, hoping to find water and food before he joined so many others who hadn't survived the cascading catastrophes.

So Machka wandered, seeking sustenance. Seeking fellowship. Seeking someone, anyone, to share the burden of survival.

But those he found still alive hadn't been interested in sharing.

One day, the farmer climbed onto his tractor, balanced his shotgun across his lap, and drove out onto the broken roadway, heading toward town. Hitched to the back of the tractor was a trailer, which he had filled with sacks of grain.

Machka took the opportunity to explore. After his initial attempt at introduction, he had avoided the house entirely, and kept clear of the barn, which stank of poisons. The granary supplied all he needed to survive, enough even to regain some of the strength he'd lost in his long, desperate trek, and the well water here was still potable, plentiful enough that the farmer would carelessly let it slop from his buckets into the depression surrounding the pump. Machka would stay long enough to recover completely, he decided, before moving on. Somewhere, surely, there was a house or village more welcoming than those he'd encountered. It couldn't all be like this.

There would be traps—Machka was sure of it and kept a wary eye for anything that might snap or spring shut as he paced the perimeter of the building. They surrounded the property, after all, and the granary, buried just beneath the surface of the soil or under drifts of dead leaves; why would the house be any different? Looking through the kitchen window, he saw a large pot on the stove. The smell of boiled meat escaped between the window and the sill, but Machka wasn't foolish enough to try to enter the building and risk being trapped inside, should the farmer return. Besides, the dog curled up beneath the kitchen table was disincentive enough. He moved on.

Circling the farmhouse, Machka approached another window, this one set in a semi-circular pit, partially below the level of the ground, and protected with bars set into the fieldstone foundation. Within, it was dark, and Machka approached, face close to the glass to overcome the sun's glare and see within. Was that movement? He came closer still.

And recoiled as something struck the glass from within.

Heart beating wildly, Machka forced himself closer. There was glass between whatever was in there and him, and if the glass gave way, iron bars. There was no danger. Still, it felt like the hairs on the back of his neck might be permanently on end.

Again, something pressed against the dirty window from within. A paw. And another. And yet another. And behind that, faces, wide-eyed and terrified, crowding the window. pawing at the glass in desperation.

Machka backed away. What had he just seen? How many kits were in there? Beyond counting—they pressed forward in a sea of dirty faces, as far as the meager light showed. Their fur was filthy and matted.

It made no sense. Why have so many if you couldn't care for them properly?

Still, there was nothing Machka could do about it. It wasn't his business anyway. They looked well-fed, at least. Which reminded him. He went to the granary and collected enough to keep himself fed for a few days and then went back to his hiding place.

The rumble of the farmer's tractor was audible before the cloud of dust and ash it kicked up became visible. Safe in his nest, Machka watched as the machine rolled up to the farmhouse, trailer in tow. It approached the back of the house, where a door was set on an angle against the house. Machka had investigated the door briefly when he'd first come here; it was important to know where any threat might potentially originate. The door was heavy—made of metal—and secured with a chain. Nothing within the house could prove a threat to Machka from that doorway.

After calling the dog, the farmer fumbled with the lock on the slanted door and unwound the chain. With a grunt, he heaved the door open. The dog stood at the top of the stairwell the open door revealed and growled.

The farmer returned to the trailer and pulled something from the bed.

Another kit.

This one was thin, emaciated, with skin that clung to its ribs and hips.

The kit screamed its fear, squirming and fighting against the ropes that bound its limbs until the farmer struck it into submission; Machka knew too well what a slap or punch or kick felt like, and he cringed at the sound of each impact. But he forced himself to watch. He needed to understand what the farmer was capable of. Just in case.

Once the kit stopped resisting, the farmer pulled a knife from his belt and cut away the ropes. Then he tucked the kit under his arm and carried it through the open door and down to join the other kits. It mewled piteously, but the farmer took no heed, and soon enough the wails faded, buried under earth and stone, behind glass and iron.

The farmer emerged from the doorway, which he closed behind him, dropping the heavy door with a deafening bang that echoed across the blighted fields. He secured it again with chain and lock, and drove the tractor into the barn. Then he and the dog returned to the farmhouse, disappearing behind the kitchen door.

It was not Machka's problem.

Machka had food. He'd stay until he was recovered, then he'd move on.

This was not his problem to solve.

A few days later, the farmer returned to the slanted door, to the basement where he kept the kits. This time he went in with the dog and a coil of rope and returned with one of the kits. This one was better fed than the one the farmer had brought home the other day. Its top legs had been secured behind its back. The dog circled it, growling, while the farmer closed and locked the basement door.

Machka had to leave his hiding place to see what happened next. The farmer walked the kit around the corner of the house, where a post had been set in the ground.

The kit cried out in fear and fled, but the dog leapt and bore it to the ground. The farmer quickly looped rope around the kit's ankles, then dragged it to the post. With a grunt, he heaved it up by the legs and hung it by the rope from a hook on the post.

The kit screamed and squirmed, but the farmer gripped it by the long fur that fell from the top of its head and held it still long enough to drag his knife across its throat.

He set a wooden bucket to catch the blood, and then cut the kit's clothes away, leaving its furless body hanging to drain.

The farmer was busy the next few days, grilling the fresh meat and slow-cooking a large stew. He salted and dried some of the meat and smoked long strings of sausages. He stretched the skin on a frame to cure.

It was no wonder that people were so quick to chase Machka away, if this was what they feared strangers might do to them. What had become of this world? Before everything had gone bad, he'd lived in a nice house where the people had three kits of their own, of different sizes. The kits were loving and gave Machka treats and toys, and played with feathers on a string with him, and barely ever pulled his tail. Machka never knew if they died in the flood that washed away their house, or if they lived, if it was to suffer like the farmer's kits. There was nothing Machka could do for his own kits, but maybe, just maybe, he could do something here.

Machka watched the farmer's actions carefully, spying through the kitchen window, or crouched amidst withered cornstalks at the edge of the field. The farmer pulled grain from the granary and water from the well to cook a gruel that he fed the kits. He filled bowls with the slop and stacked them on a small table beside a door on the far wall of the kitchen. The door had a slot through which he passed the bowls, one by one. The meat he kept for himself and the dog.

The kitchen itself was full of dangerous things. Blades of all sizes, from massive cleavers to small, sharp paring knives, hung from magnets on the walls and littered the tables and counters. And there was no shortage of guns — shotguns and pistols, long rifles and short-muzzled rifles with long blocks clipped to them.

When Machka was not spying on the farmer, he was prowling the grounds, searching for traps. These he found in abundance. Most of them consisted of nasty snapping metal jaws with jagged teeth. They were triggered, Machka learned, when something stepped on a plate between the two jaws. Or if someone dropped a rock from high enough to simulate a paw coming down.

Most of the traps were hidden under brush or dried leaves and then attached with a chain to a tree trunk, or with a spike hammered firmly into the ground. Sometimes, however, the spike was not so firmly embedded after all. That, Machka decided, was convenient. And useful.

Now, to set a plan in motion, before another kit was murdered.

Not every trap needed bait—the ones the farmer set certainly didn't, just set them where someone was likely to walk—but the trap Machka was setting did. He found his bait in the granary. Machka knew that farmers weren't nearly as fond of rodents as he was, so after his preparations were made, he went hunting. This time, instead of eating his prey, he left it unharmed, carrying it by the nape of the neck to the kitchen door. Mice, he knew from experience, could squeeze through very narrow gaps. He dropped the mouse at the foot of the door and hissed at it menacingly. Obligingly, it scuttled under the door.

Machka swiped at the disappearing tail, just to give it more incentive.

It worked. A few seconds later the dog barked in alarm. Claws scampered on wooden floors. Furniture shifted and crashed, and the farmer shouted angrily as glass and ceramics shattered.

Machka leapt up onto the windowsill to watch.

Frantic to escape the dog, the mouse had scurried up the farmer's leg and leapt onto the kitchen table. The dog followed, spilling food and drink everywhere. The mouse jumped again, narrowly escaping the dog's slavering jaws, catching on the farmer's shirt. The dog pounced and all three of them crashed to the floor.

The mouse squirmed out from under the farmer and ran for the door. Machka felt his tail twitch. He leapt down from his perch and waited by the door, swiping at the whiskers as they appeared. The mouse backed up and disappeared, just as a heavy footfall slammed the floor on the other side of the door. The farmer issued a cry of triumph.

Machka backed into the shadows and waited.

A moment later, the door swung open. The farmer stood outlined in the doorway, holding the mouse's limp body by the tail. He took a step.

The trap Machka had dragged over snapped shut.

Crying out, the farmer fell forward.

Machka pounced. Not on the mouse, but on the man's face, scratching and clawing at his eyes.

Barking furiously, the dog lunged, snapping at Machka. But Machka was prepared, leaping away at the last moment, and the dog's jaws clamped on the man's face instead.

Tempting as it was to turn and watch, Machka knew that would be the death of him. Running as fast as he could, Machka raced toward the line of trees. The dog raced after him.

Despite having a head start, the dog's longer legs gave him an edge. Machka hoped he hadn't miscalculated. The woods grew close, but so did the dog. Machka leapt up onto a fallen log and then another long jump out beyond it. Snarling, the dog jumped farther, clearing the log entirely, and then screaming as the trap on the other side of the log snapped shut on his front legs.

Machka held his tail proudly as he sauntered past the dog and hopped back over the log, but once out of the dog's sight, he hurried back to the farmhouse. He'd vanquished his foes, yes, but the farmer wasn't done yet, and he could still retreat back into his farmhouse and lock himself in.

When he got back, the farmer had gotten his leg out of the trap and was trying to pull himself to his feet. But the leg bent like a second knee, and with a cry he fell again.

There was very little time. If Machka couldn't free the kits before the farmer crawled in and got his hands on his weapons, the plan would fail. Machka sprinted as fast as he could. He imagined a dog slavering at his heels, rather than running toward danger. He leapt over the farmer and dashed across the kitchen.

The door with the feeding slot was held shut with a wooden plank that fitted into squared hooks on the wall and the door. If Machka could move the board...

He jumped up on the small table beside the door. Yes, he could reach the board from here. The tabletop was made of a soft wood, and Machka's claws found easy purchase. A good grip to push against. Using all his strength, he pushed and pushed, and bit by bit, the board moved.

The farmer had dragged himself inside, approaching the kitchen table, where the shotgun lay amidst the spilled drinks and stew.

Machka could hear the kits on the other side of the door. Sometimes they pressed against it, making it impossible to move the board. He wondered what they might be thinking. Had they watched through the feeding slot? What might they have seen?

The farmer was using a chair to pull himself up. Soon, he'd have the shotgun.

Machka hated shotguns. He still had scars on his flank, where he hadn't entirely escaped the spray of pellets from one. Sometimes, he felt the metal scrape against his bones, and he couldn't bear to sleep in a way that put pressure on that side.

Suddenly, the board slid the rest of the way out of the slot. Machka pitched forward, losing his balance. He scrambled to catch the edge of the table and failed. Just a tail-length away, the board teetered precariously, slowly tilting to one side. Tipping off the edge of the table, Machka fell to the floor, twisting to land on his feet, and then the board fell across his back. He sprang away from it with a cry, just in time to avoid the door as it burst open.

The kits rushed out the door, filling the kitchen with more feet than Machka had ever avoided before. They reached the shotgun before the farmer did.

Shotguns, Machka knew, were loud. They were even louder indoors.

It was nice, Machka thought, to live in a house again.

The kits had decided to stay, though not in the basement. They filled the other rooms in the farmhouse instead, sleeping three or four to a room, ordered by size, which, Machka figured, was probably related to age.

Working together, the kits had brought a small part of the fields back to life, watering daily from the well. They built lightweight wooden frames woven with dried corn stalks to provide shade from the unrelenting sun, moving them to different parts of the field during the day to ensure that none of the crops withered away.

It wasn't much, but it was enough to replenish the granary at the end of the season.

Machka, for his part, kept the granary from being overrun by rats and mice, and was never lacking in pets and play. When he was in the mood.

Lister

SUNDAY IN THE PARK WITH SPOT
Keith R.A. DeCandido

"Can I hear a story? Please?"

"All right—*one* story, and that's it. Then you must sleep."

"Just one?"

"Yes, just one—and be thankful for that."

"But—Okay, just one, then."

"You promise to go right to sleep after that?"

"Yes, ma'am."

"Good. In that case, I will tell you a story that takes place in a mythical land called 'The Bronx.'"

"Where's the Bronx?"

"It's in a magical city known as New York. The Bronx is the northernmost region of that fair city, populated by a good portion of the Folk, as well as many other strange beings—fish and fowl, mammal and invertebrate. Perhaps the most baffling are the ones called humans. They are charming, peculiar creatures, who believe themselves to be the only intelligent people in the world when they in fact have very little to do with the day-to-day reality."

"Why do they think that?"

"That is one of the great mysteries. However, they do perform several useful functions—they provide food and shelter for many of the Folk, and they also have produced some remarkable healers. In particular, they have done much to aid the cat and dog population."

"Cats make sense, but why dogs?"

"That is another of the great mysteries, but this one has a likely solution: dogs are fiercely loyal. Humans tend to reward such behavior."

"But cats aren't loyal to *anything*."

"True, but cats treat those who provide for them well. Humans are not particularly bright specimens, and they probably mistake that kind treatment for the same loyalty they observe in dogs."

"That makes sense."

"Now please, don't interrupt anymore."

"Sorry."

"Our story takes us to one house in a neighborhood in the Bronx known as Riverdale. Many Folk lived in this region, including the Chief Chaos Wrangler, Mittens. On one fine Sunday afternoon—a day when most humans remain at home to care for their domiciles and tend to the needs of the Folk—Mittens received a sign.

"Now Chaos Wranglers, you must understand, cannot always predict when they will need to ply their trade. By its very nature, Chaos is random and indefinable, and so the times when it must be curtailed can come at the most inconvenient moments.

"On this day, Mittens found himself with the usual indicator that there would be a shift in the Chaotic Winds—an itch behind his left ear—and that he would need to move quickly. The first thing he had to do was confirm the shift by tracing the sigils.

"Naturally, Mittens's humans did not understand this behavior. They were a pair who had mated, male and female, named Bob and Sue."

"Those are really weird names. So's Mittens, actually."

"Humans have very bizarre customs regarding nomenclature. Unfortunately, the rules of hospitality state that the one providing shelter also provides the names for those who dwell under that shelter—no matter how ridiculous those names might be. So it has always been."

"That's a silly rule."

"What did I say about interruptions? Especially foolish ones."

"You didn't say anything about foolish ones."

"But I did tell you not to interrupt. Now be silent.

"Sue saw that Mittens was tracing the sigils, but humans are not terrifically bright creatures, and so she said, 'Oh, Mittens, what's gotten into you *this* time?'

"From another room, Bob said, 'What's the little guy doing now, sweetie?'

"'Just his usual gadding about. I swear, I don't know what gets into that cat sometimes.'

"'You did feed him, right?'

"In a long-suffering tone, Sue said, '*Yes*, dear, of *course* I fed him.'

"'Just checking. You want me to take out the pooch?'"

"What's a pooch?"

"If you stopped interrupting, I'd tell you. 'Pooch' is a human term for a dog. You see, Bob and Sue sheltered a dog as well as a cat. While Mittens lived inside their abode, their dog, who was called Spot, spent most of his time in the outdoor expanse behind their shelter. He had his own small shelter, which Sue had constructed for him. The humans, whatever their other failings, are fine craftspeople.

"In response to Bob's question, Sue said, 'Let me give him his food, first, then you can take him out.'

"'Good—that gives me time for a shower.'

"Before you interrupt again, I will explain—a shower is something else the humans have built. It is a device they use to groom themselves by pouring water on their persons."

"Pouring water? That's icky! Why do that on purpose?"

"It is yet another mystery about humans. May I continue without interruption?"

"Sorry."

"Sue poured food into the receptacle designated for Spot. In his shelter behind the abode, Spot heard the distinctive clank of the dry food against the metal of the receptacle and immediately forgot whatever he was doing and ran for the abode, with thoughts only of food dancing in his head.

"Meanwhile, Mittens had been paying very close attention to the exchange between Sue and Bob even as he collated the data from his tracing of the sigils. The news that Bob was planning to take Spot out heartened Mittens, as it meant he himself would not need to sneak out. Mittens had clandestinely left the shelter a few times, and it only served to worry the humans unnecessarily. They tended to obsess over Mittens's safety when he wasn't in their domicile—as if cats could not survive on their own away from their humans. Still, Mittens knew that Bob and Sue's hearts were in the right place, misguided though their fears might be, and he was loath to put them in such a position.

"Spot would make that unnecessary. Though there were attendant risks in trusting a dog.

"After Spot ran in and shoved his face into his receptacle—dogs have *no* sense of finesse when it comes to matters culinary; it's rather embarrassing, really—Mittens finished grooming himself and waited for Sue to finish patting Spot on the head and saying, 'Good dog, Spot.' Humans tend to praise Folk for doing what comes naturally for some odd reason.

"Once Sue left, Mittens approached Spot while the latter was gorging himself. 'I have a task for you,' the cat said.

"The dog looked up from his food. 'A job? I like jobs. Jobs are fun. Thank you for trusting me with a job! What's the job mean? What do I do? When do I do it?'

"'I will tell you,' Mittens said patiently. 'Bob will be taking you to the park for a run.'

"'A run? I love runs! Runs are great fun! I get to run this way and that, and sometimes if I'm really lucky, I get to chase a stick or a ball! I love doing that!'

"'Yes, and you should enjoy it as much as you want—especially as it will make Bob happy as well.'

"'You think so?' Spot seemed thrilled by the very idea. 'That'd be great!'

"'However, you must do something else.'

"Spot was confused for a moment, then said, 'Right! The job! I remember now, you want me to do a job!' Spot then realized he was parched and padded over to the water dish. After lapping up some water, he turned back to Mittens. 'I will do this job for you.'

"With that he started to walk off, but Mittens stepped in front of the dog before he could go out the door. 'I haven't told you the job yet, Spot.'

"'Oh, right! I'll need that, won't I? Okay, tell me what the job is so I can do it for you.'

"Grateful that he now had Spot's undivided attention, Mittens explained the job. 'When Bob takes you to the park, you must find the squirrel named Tail-Drop.'"

"That's a different name. Are the squirrels' humans smarter?"

"I'm afraid not. For whatever reason, humans do not shelter squirrels. They are self-sheltering by nature and also tend to prefer the outdoors more often than not. As a result, they choose their own names. However, it also makes them useful helpmeets for the Chaos Wranglers.

"Mittens explained to Spot: 'You must find Tail-Drop and then tell her to trace the Order Sigil at the World Tree at precisely the time of sunset.'

"'Order Sigil, World Tree, sunset. Got it. Won't be any problem. I'll do just what you ask, Mittens, youbetcha.'

"'There's one important thing.' Mittens hesitated then, because too much information might be rough on the dog, but he needed to know this. 'The information can be passed on to any gray squirrel you meet, in case you don't find Tail-Drop. But it's very important that you do *not* share this with the black squirrel.'

"'Not the black squirrel.' Spot nodded. 'No problem. I'll do it. Youbetcha.'

"Mittens was concerned, but Spot had a good heart and a noble soul. He would do the right thing.

"When Spot was done eating, and after Bob had altered his protective covering, he attached a tether to Spot's collar and took him out of the abode to a grassland that the humans had named Ewen Park."

"Why a tether?"

"More of that worrying that humans indulge in so much. They fear that their Folk will be endangered if they are not physically linked. Bob, however, only kept the tether on until they arrived at Ewen Park. This grassland has several sections, one of which is bordered by fences and intended for dogs to roam free. Most humans don't have wide-open spaces for dogs to run in, and they are Folk who enjoy such, so some humans will bring their dogs to such grasslands.

"For a while, Spot was happy to run after a stick that Bob would toss across the grassland, intending for Spot to retrieve it. And this action made Spot happy, as Bob was happy, and he got to run free.

"After the fifth time he retrieved the stick, the sight of a squirrel running across reminded Spot that he had a job to do. Unfortunately, Spot found he couldn't remember the specifics, beyond the fact that he had to talk to a squirrel.

"He thought back to his conversation with Mittens even as he ran to fetch the stick another time. For sure, he knew he had to tell a squirrel to trace the sigils for Order at the World Tree. Spot had no idea which one *was* the World Tree, but he also knew that such matters were not for dogs. That was the type of thing cats worried about—dogs had much more important jobs, like fetching sticks and running in circles.

"Finally, Spot remembered something very important—the black squirrel. Spot didn't know the squirrel's name, but there was only one black squirrel that made its home in Ewen Park, and Spot now knew with complete certainty that the black squirrel was the one he had to talk to. Mittens had made a very special point of it.

"Unfortunately, the black squirrel was nowhere to be found. Spot kept searching every time he fetched the stick, but no black squirrel. Plenty of gray ones—including one who looked familiar, though Spot couldn't for the life of him remember who it was—but no sign of the black.

"Bob started talking to another human by the name of Louie, who sheltered Buford and Cello. Spot always liked Buford, who was big and friendly and loud. Cello was small and annoying, though, and Spot didn't like him very much.

"Spot started thinking about how much he liked Buford and didn't like Cello, until he caught sight of a pigeon, flying down toward the benches where humans sometimes sat and threw food to the ground. Although Spot found pigeons to be vile Folk, he also knew that they saw things nobody else did from the air. So he went over to one pigeon and asked her, 'Have you seen the black squirrel?'

"The pigeon gazed up at him with confusion. 'What are you talking about, Spot? Why do you want to talk to Fan-Tail?'

"Spot remembered that that was the black squirrel's name, and that he never liked that name. But he never liked Mittens as a name, either. To answer the pigeon's question, Spot said, 'Mittens told me to!'

"'I doubt that very much,' the pigeon said, cooing with laughter.

"'He did too! Mittens was very specific! He told me to tell Fan-Tail to trace the Order Tree in the Sigils World! Or, rather, the Order Sigils in the World Tree!'

"Cautiously, because she didn't want to anger the dog that was so much bigger than her, the pigeon said, 'I doubt that very much, Spot. Mittens is the Chaos Wrangler. Fan-Tail is an agent of Chaos. He is absolutely the wrong person to give this information to.'

"'Hmph.' Spot looked down his muzzle at the pigeon. 'That shows what *you* know, you stupid pigeon. Mittens was very precise and made sure to mention Fan-Tail *by name*.' Spot knew that was a slight fib, as Mittens hadn't given the black squirrel's name, but the pigeon didn't need to know that. She just needed to tell Spot where Fan-Tail *was*.

"But the pigeon was much smarter than the dog."

"Wouldn't take a lot."

"You'd been doing so well with the interruptions."

"Sorry, but the dog is just so *dumb*."

"It's not the dog's fault. It is in their nature to be easily distracted. Still, Spot was Mittens's best option, despite the risks. After all, time was of the essence. It was already midafternoon, and if Tail-Drop didn't trace the Order Sigils in the World Tree, the consequences would be very dire indeed.

"In any event, the pigeon was smarter than the dog, but the dog didn't appreciate that. Pigeons are not among the birds sheltered by humans."

"Why would anybody shelter a *bird*?"

"Oh, plenty of humans do. It's another of their mysteries — they shelter beings whose purpose is to fly through the air and then put them in cages so they cannot roam free. But pigeons, for whatever reason, are not among those they so imprison. In fact, most humans view them as necessary evils, not appreciating their value as scouts and observers among the Folk. They are always watching, and when necessary marking those items or people that warrant further attention from the Folk."

"So then what happened? Did the dog find the black squirrel?"

"Sadly, yes. Though the pigeon did everything she could to dissuade him, Spot was convinced that Fan-Tail was the squirrel he needed to talk to rather than the one he should avoid. So when he caught sight of the black squirrel, he ran to him as fast as his paws could take him.

"Bob was engaged in his conversation with Lou and did not notice Spot's bolting. The pigeon took matters into her own wings by flying close to Bob's head, which distracted the human and enabled him to observe Spot running away from the fenced area and down toward the paved pathway that humans use to walk through the park."

"Why would anyone pave a park? Or is that another one of those human mysteries?"

"Are you continuing to ask ridiculous questions in order to avoid sleep?"

"No! Honest, no! Is it just that humans don't make sense?"

"Yes. Humans are incomprehensible and not very bright. It's usually best to simply accept the offerings they provide and otherwise try to ignore them.

"Now then, Spot had sighted Fan-Tail and so ran toward him. The black squirrel was surprised — he was usually shunned by the canine population, but this one was galumphing toward him with enthusiasm usually reserved for retrieving a round ball thrown by a human.

Fan-Tail twitched his nose in anticipation. He saw one of two possibilities: The first was that the dog had switched sides and wanted to help Fan-Tail. The second, and more likely, was that the dog had made a terrible mistake.

"'Hello! You're Fan-Tail, right? Aren't'cha? I hope so! I've got something I need to tell you!'

"'Yes, that's me,' Fan-Tail said. 'I'm that squirrel. Yes, I am. Please go ahead. Tell me. Go on.'

"'This is *really* important! I've got a message for you, and it's from *Mittens*, the Chaos Wrangler.'

"The black squirrel's nose twitched again. It was definitely option number two: Mittens would never send an emissary to talk to Fan-Tail. They were mortal enemies, serving opposite masters. The black squirrel was on the side of chaos, after all. He assured Spot, 'I'm listening. Go ahead. Tell me. I'm rapt.'

"Spot paused a second. He knew this was very important to Mittens, and he hated the idea of letting anyone down, so he wanted to make sure he got the message *exactly* right. 'Okay, here it is—you need to go to the World Tree and trace the Otter Sigils.'

"Fan-Tail managed to resist the urge to rub his claws together and bob his tail up and down. It wouldn't do for this dog, regardless of how dim he seemed, to be aware of just how spectacularly he had screwed up. 'World Tree. Otter Sigils. Good. When?'

"That brought Spot up short. 'When?'

"'Yes,' the squirrel said. 'When? Need to know. Tell me. When?'

"Spot panicked. He couldn't remember that part. Most of it, he remembered. He remembered that Mittens told him to tell the black squirrel about the sigils and the World Tree and that he had to fetch the stick every time Bob threw it and that he was hungry again. He remembered all of that. But when had fallen right out of his head.

"Just then, Bob cried out, 'Spot! What're you doing over there? C'mon, boy, we gotta get home before it gets dark!'

"Those words brought it home for Spot. 'Midnight! I remember now, Mittens specifically said that at the precise moment of total darkness—right at midnight. That's it.'

"This time, Fan-Tail didn't bother stopping himself from rubbing his claws together. The stupid dog had played right into his hands. Obviously, the Chaos Wrangler had divined the black squirrel's spell-casting tomorrow morning and planned to counter it at midnight with the Otter Sigils. Fan-Tail would simply go to the World Tree at midnight and trace the sigils himself. As an agent of chaos, the sigils would have a much different effect if he traced them than they would from one of those annoying gray squirrels."

"There are really Otter Sigils?"

"Of course. Why do you think that otters swim in such precise patterns?"

"Then how can the black squirrel trace them at a tree?"

"If you stop interrupting, you'll find out."

"I'm sorry."

"Now then—Bob put the tether back on Spot when he caught up to the dog, and the pair of them went back to Bob and Sue's shelter. Spot was barking happily, thrilled that he had fulfilled his mission."

"But he didn't! I'm sorry to interrupt again, but Spot *didn't* fulfill his mission! He helped Chaos win!"

"What have I told you about judging a story before hearing its end?"

"That isn't the end of the story?"

"No. You see, Mittens is no fool. One does not become Chaos Wrangler without learning a few tricks and being aware of your surroundings. You see, what Mittens saw was that Fan-Tail had planned to cast a spell that would bring chaos into the Bronx—and the Bronx has enough of that as it is."

"If it was so dangerous, then why entrust the dog to convey so critical a message?"

"Because the message was not as critical as Spot was lead to believe. When Bob brought Spot back, the dog immediately found Mittens and started running around the cat, encircling him several times. 'I did it! I did it, I did it, I did it! I told that black squirrel exactly what to do, *just* like you asked! He'll be at the World Tree at midnight tracing the Otter Sigils!'

"Mittens meowed affectionately, and said, 'Well done.'"

"But it wasn't well done! It was all wrong! Dogs are stupid!"

"Yes, dogs are. They mean well, but they are forgetful and easily distracted and tend to mangle what they've been given. Which was exactly why Mittens gave the instructions to Spot that he did, with special mention of Fan-Tail—he knew that the dog would muck it up. That Spot used Otter Sigils instead of Order Sigils made the jest even greater, because the only way to re-create Otter Sigils on land is to writhe in the dirt, an amusing visual image that Mittens would treasure."

"So Spot was *supposed* to tell the black squirrel instead of the gray one?"

"Not necessarily. If he got it right, no harm would be done. If Tail-Drop did trace the Order Sigils on the World Tree at sunset — or at midnight, for that matter — it would only strengthen the counterspell that Mittens himself was going to cast at dawn to stop Fan-Tail. But now the black squirrel would be distracted by Spot's news and be even easier for Mittens to defeat."

"Mittens is a very clever cat."

"He has to be in order to be a proper Chaos Wrangler. So that is how Mittens was able to use Spot to stop Fan-Tail from bringing more chaos into the world."

"What about the pigeon?"

"What?"

"The pigeon? What happened to her?"

"Oh, eventually, Mittens was able to explain to her what was going on. The pigeon was not pleased that she had gone to all that effort for nothing, but Mittens assured her that her objections to Spot only reinforced Spot's determination to do the right thing — that is to say, the *wrong* thing, by talking to the black squirrel. That mollified the pigeon, and she continued to do her job of scouting and observing and marking those things that warranted attention.

"And that ends the story. The sun's all the way up, so it's time for you to wash up and go to sleep. Make sure you groom between each one of your claws before going to bed."

"I will. Thank you for the story!"

"You're welcome, little kitten."

Kaylee and Louie

WHEN THEY CHOOSE YOU
Danielle Ackley-McPhail

We all joke about the CDS… the Cat Distribution System. There are memes and videos about it everywhere. I'm sure you've seen them.

Before that term was even a thing, we got flagged by a very determined puss. See, we lived in Queens, in an apartment over a storefront, accessed by a little fenced-in alleyway leading to a side door that led up to our apartment. Living on a busy street, Liberty Avenue, we didn't see much wildlife.

Until we did.

One day I came home from work to an orange tabby hanging out on our stoop. For a solid week it sat there or on the pavement leading to the back of the building. There when we went to work, there when we returned. But the apartment wasn't ours, technically, and my mother-in-law had already made her views known on bringing any more cats into the house. She'd already allowed one (which she brought in herself) but that was more than enough for her.

But you know, even the hardest hearts have a soft spot somewhere. After a week of looking up at us hopefully from below, in reasonably pleasant weather, that tabby's situation took a turn for the worse. The mother of all storms hit. Torrential downpour doesn't even begin to describe it.

And yet that tabby — I'd named him Alley by then — still sat on that stoop looking up. Like he had no doubt where he was meant to be. When I came home from work and saw him still sitting there, drenched, my heart just twisted up for him.

But it wasn't my call.

I will tell you, though… that bit I was saying about the hardest hearts…

The moment I walked up the stairs to our apartment I hear from the other room.

"If he's coming in, he's going to the vet first!"

When you know, you know, and Alley knew.

Alley

MERVAT IN THE MAIDEN'S TOWER
Jeff Young

THE AEROFLOT SWAYING IN THE BREEZE, I CONSIDERED CONSTANTINOPLE below me, visible between my wrinkled old toes where they jutted out from my sandals. I had never seen the city from such a height. The air was for the rich or the couriers carrying the words and will of the rich. My tasks were much more earthbound. Let those with grand purpose flit about overhead, little Mervat would rather be saving lives below.

The crossroads of the East and West was somewhat visible through the smoke from homes and businesses that rose like sooty djinn above the cedar-shrouded hills counterpointed by the upthrust minarets of the mosques. Constantinople's veins crawled with locomotives chugging their way toward the center as ships plowed their way through her arteries to port. The heart of the Ottoman Empire pulsed to the sound of crying gulls, the ringing bells of the Byzantine churches, and the call to prayer of the muezzins. I struggled to keep my greying hair under the shawl I'd tossed over my shoulders and then pulled over my head, wondering all the while what use I was, the matron of the hospital founded by Florence Nightengale, to the harbormaster, that he would summon me so?

The lift bag of the small airship snapped like a sail, and I jerked in the harness like a fool. My pilot was an ancient fellow, though spry enough to pedal the great fan beneath the carriage through its rotations, and also occasionally to stamp the bellows to keep the coal burner lit under the lift bag. I truly wondered at his stamina, but the lines of prayer flags hanging from the prow and his features convinced me that his Himalayan background were suited to such an elevation. With mustaches like a walrus, yellowed by either a smoking or turmeric habit, he occasionally turned around to follow the trail of little streamers of sparks flying backward from the brazier like shooting stars; perhaps only slightly concerned they might set me alight. The scent of whale oil that kept the gears from squeaking hung about us in a haze broken only by the occasional breezes. I held my shawl over my nose lest I sneeze.

With a sigh and a wary gaze, I considered the many clouds that filled the sky. Not exactly pleasant weather, and certainly not improved by the smoke from industry. For a moment the haze parted, and to my delight, sunlight flicked across the waters of the Bosphorus like a lightning flash, vanishing just as quickly. Once again, I was drawn back to the clouds, their dark roiling undersides all too close. Something more seemed to swirl within those condensed vapors… I wondered, peering upward. The vision came over me suddenly.

Stairs ascended into darkness, each anchored by the glow of two green points of light.

I shook my head until the image no longer persisted, my heartbeat erratic, my breathing shallow. I set myself the task of finding inner calm. Breathing in one nostril and out the other, I balanced myself; so much easier than if it had happened while I attended to a patient. Visions, no matter how strange, were not to be feared. My grandmother, who raised me after my parents vanished under mysterious circumstances, had made sure I understood that. She'd flipped through ancient books pointing out passages about the Sibyls of ancient Greece, as well as dreams brought on during the day by the gods of many religions. I still remember fondly her introducing me to many world beliefs: Greek, Etruscan, Celtic. I remember the symbols of their resulting religions, like the bull of Mithraism and the eternal Zoroastrian flame. Now those very same volumes rest in places of honor upon my own shelves.

Pulling the shawl tighter about my shoulders to dispel the chill that settled there, I contemplated the image brought to me in the vision: darkness and green lights. What could it mean? I found it difficult to see this as the gift from the gods that my grandmother always insisted it was. It had been years since I'd had a vision, and the timing definitely concerned me. In consideration of my current destination, perhaps it was best to set aside these thoughts for the moment.

Today certainly held many questions. What did the harbormaster want from me? And what was that looming shape on the horizon? Could it be the Chinese dirigible of late whispered about on the streets? Why were they not allowed to land? Stuck repeating this circular loop, they loomed overhead, a threatening presence whose shadows darkened the streets below, making the antlike people stop and point at the sky, unlike the silvery hulls of other trade dirigibles tied up at the farthest northern portions of the port, away from the shipping lanes.

With an unsettling jerk, the aeroflot began its ungainly descent to the roof of the harbormaster's offices. My head spun as we spiraled downward. Round and round, we dropped lower, with stomach-flipping hitches, as the pilot toggled the flaps on the side of his vehicle to vent hot air. The landing snapped my chin to my chest as the aeroflot's struts thumped down on the rooftop.

Fortunately, I didn't have to pay for the journey. I untied the restraining belt and jumped to the roof; dust fountaining up around my sandals. Before I could turn about, the brush of air from the motive fan rushed over me, and the aeroflot was away on its next journey. A door opened ahead of me, and a figure with a cloth over their mouth gestured me forward. I was only given a few moments to shake the dust from myself before being ushered into the august presence of Erhan, the Master of Haydarpaşa Port.

Seated in a high-backed wooden chair with an antelope-hide seat, I stared into the depths of the strong tea that the harbormaster had given me, waiting until he deigned to speak. After enough time had passed to try my patience, I took a full sip of tea and then gently cleared my throat. The rustling of papers came to a halt.

Before Erhan could speak, the entire office began to vibrate in sympathy with the fans of an airship passing overhead. The teacups jumped, the painted tiles on the wall chattered, and the Damascus steel kukri hanging over Erhan's desk tipped forward. With a gesture that spoke of both repetition and frustration, he reached up and pushed the blade back onto the hanger bolts without looking. Our gazes swung toward the window with its view of the blue waters of the Bosporus. The shadow of the *Alpasian* stretched out above the buildings of Constantinople. The third ship of the Ottoman fleet had arrived. Even as it joined its sister ships, the *Alpasian* was dwarfed by the floating monstrosity that was the Chinese Khongqi Long class dirigible.

Dark eyes wide, Erhan stabbed his finger toward the Chinese ship as if he could pierce its side and save the trouble of an unwelcome visitor. "These infidels and their impatience will cost us. No one wants a war with their nation, but they insist on docking without following protocols."

Completely surprising me, the harbormaster leaned forward over the desk conspiratorially and said, "There are rumors that the Black Death has come to the Empire of the Sun, and that their navy flees to safe havens."

He paused, almost as if he wasn't certain what to say next, fingers drumming on the table. "That beast up there is running on its last fumes and their crew is starving, but I will not be responsible for their bringing the plague to my city." Realizing how far he had leaned toward me; he sat back into his carved wooden chair and straightened his tunic.

Another stab of his finger; this time in my direction, made me flinch. "This is your part in things. As the head of the hospital, we will need you to assess the state of the Chinese crew. To aid in this, a temporary docking rig is being assembled and will be towed out to the Kýz Kulesi. What is it that the tourists call it?"

"It's known as the Maiden's Tower, sir. Constructed by the Byzantine Emperor Comnenus. The legends say he sequestered his daughter there after an oracle prophesied that she would die of a venomous snakebite on her eighteenth birthday. Unfortunately, a snake crawled into a basket of fruit brought in for the birthday celebration and…" I trailed off noticing the raised eyebrows of my host. "Sorry, legends and mythology are a pleasure. You were talking about a docking rig?" I prompted.

Shaking his head, Erhan continued, "Once installed and anchored to the island, it will allow the Khongqi Long ship to lower crew for review and for us to raise supplies to the ship. You will inspect the crew and make a determination of the state of their health. If necessary, you may use the Scudari Barracks for their quarantine, as your mentor, Ms. Nightengale, once did. We can also make water and food available to the crew. But no one, not a single person or creature, is to land from that ship until you clear them. So, Ms. Mervat, that is your task. You will, of course, need to take several nurses to aid you. I will supply you with a squad of harbor watchmen to ensure there are no military misunderstandings. Ultimately, the decision will be yours to make concerning their fate." After a hard stare, Erhan slid a pile of paperwork across his broad desk to me, took a slurp of tea, and cleared his throat, before turning back to glare at the Chinese ship floating above his port.

That, I supposed, was that. Grasping the papers and my nerves as best I could, I stood to see myself out; knees popping in protest as I struggled to my feet. I shuffled my way past the giant silver tea urn at the entrance to Erhan's office and through the door. It was a long trip as I wound my way down the stairs, occasionally stepping to one side to let a port employee with armloads of paperwork pass me by. At my age, a fall down those stairs would bring a quick end to my career. Well, I'd wanted to show them I could still do important things. If only Ms. Nightingale could see me now. Glancing back, I wondered if perhaps Erhan's exclamation was actually a sigh of relief that this was no longer his responsibility. Coming out into the main hall, I found a seat on a bench to consider the paperwork I'd acquired.

Here was a requisition for a boat. That was immediately helpful. Here was also a requisition for a squad of watchmen. Lastly, here was a writ of credit to pay for whatever was necessary. This was quite a bit. In fact, it might slow down the process of getting me to the point of diagnosing the crewmen. I closed my eyes. It was only for a moment, and it felt good. I forced them open once more, and gathering as much determination as I could muster, started for the doorway.

At the bottom of the stairs outside the office, I acquired a shadow. A very familiar familial shadow. "Whatever it is Kurnaz, the answer is, no." I planted a hand on my hip and stared at him.

"What? A cousin cannot stop to see about the welfare of their relation? Truly, do not ascribe evil where none exists."

"So, there is no reason at all you happen to be skulking about the Harbormaster's Office?"

"I resent that. I am most certainly not skulking about. I am here because you are just done with meeting one of the most important people in Constantinople, who has, no doubt, given you a task of great significance. Such an occurrence can only mean that you are in need of assistance, and Mervat, who can you trust, if you cannot trust your own blood?"

I stared at him and let the moment draw out, my scowl lingering as my mind worked at this latest surprise. The reality was that I needed someone to look after the details and let me do my work. No, I wasn't going to, there was no way I'd ever... it made... I sighed. In reality, it made perfect sense to let my busybody cousin deal with the parts that I didn't wish to, but we were going to do things my way.

"No."

"What? No consideration at all? How can you just throw away such generosity on my part?"

I had him now, but I would need to seal the deal, so I explained what was required. After I finished, he thew up his hands, huffed, and turned away from me to walk down the street. I stayed where I was. This was all part of the dance, like haggling over a rug in the marketplace.

"It's fine. I understand that it's too much for you. Maybe if I have something simpler, next time I will seek you out." He stopped in his tracks. "Look it's perfectly straightforward. You would be acting in my name to make sure that—" I started.

"It's nurses. What do I want to do with nurses? Unless… is Salome still—you know of whom I speak, the one with eyes like deep wells—" He looked back over his shoulder at me, smoothing his thinning hair across a broad forehead.

"I will choose the nurses. You will organize the watchmen. You will get the boat. You will make sure that they can set up the docking tower. That is quite a bit of responsibility. Perhaps I should find someone else…"

Kurnaz spun about, retracing his steps to lunge forward and catch at my arm, "Now, cousin, do not be hasty in your choices. I am certain you could find someone willing to deal with all of this, and you do have to admit it is quite a bit. But—and consider this carefully—who else really would be foolish enough to get involved without a hefty payment?"

I turned away, so he couldn't see my grin. I wiped it from my face as swiftly as possible. To catch Kurnaz one only had to use the right bait. Now that I had him though, I would have to play him like a fish on the line, for his interest was sure to wane over time. At the moment, the promise of authority and money would work. "Here is the writ for the boat. It's best we start there so that we know what we are walking into. Kýz Kulesi hasn't been used in years, and we're going to have to turn it into a dock *and* a medical facility. Contact me as soon as possible." I didn't need to look up to remind him of the threat overhead.

"Cousin, we didn't discuss payment…"

I shook my head at him, "You will be paid, that's all."

"Fine, then meet me at the docks in an hour," Kurnaz said confidently.

My sharp look helped him to reconsider. "No, I will see you after midday."

"Fine," his tone indicated understanding, and a little contrition.

That was perfect for me. It gave me time to pack and collect my bag of medicines and tools. Then it was across the water to the Tower.

I stepped around the dog drinking from a dip in the paving stones intentionally designed to collect water for such purpose and looked up to the doorway of my hospital. Before continuing, I turned back to gaze at the cur's brindled fur. There were days when I loved living in a city that carefully looked out for its animal inhabitants, but wasn't it strange to see so many dogs and no cats? *Ah well*, I thought, *it is as Grandmother said, "Men lead dogs where they like, and cats go where* they *like."*

Smiling and shaking my head, I reached out for the railing to ascend the few steps into the building. When my hand clasped the cold metal, it sent a shock through me. The sounds of the city faded in and out. All of my senses dulled save that of my inner eye. Again, so soon? After so long without? I swayed as a beam of sunlight breaking through the overhead haze caught my gaze and sent my perceptions elsewhere.

Over a wall, the water surged back and forth, and from the skies fell metal and flames that hissed as they struck the waves.

My heart stuttered like it had missed a beat. At my sharp intake of breath, the dog turned and looked at me. Its small whine of concern brought me back to myself. I'd slumped against the smooth wall, my cheek resting on the cool stone. Blinking rapidly, I pushed myself upright, rocking back onto my feet to straighten my dress and nurse's apron. I was relieved this episode had gone unnoticed by anyone from the hospital. I needed my people to trust me, especially if we might be headed into dangerous circumstances. I couldn't appear weak or incapacitated.

Even so, I trembled, my belly twisting like an agitated nest of snakes. What had I seen? An airship crashing? How could I know, and just which divine entity had I to thank for sharing such cryptic signs? Focusing on my breathing, I calmed myself with the assurance that such glimpses showed me only one *possible* future. Grandmother always said, "People were not meant to live in the future, only in the now. The now was a cart to which humans were tethered. Sometimes you rode the cart and sometimes you pulled the cart." If only I could find a way to *steer*.

Shaking my head, I pulled open the hospital door. Scents of astringents and alcohol replaced the smoke, spice, and other street aromas. Inside waited the organized chaos that I'd made my own for the better part of my career. It took only a few moments to set people to gather the necessary supplies and then briefly settle at my desk to collect my thoughts.

I'd seen the island from a distance my whole life and was always too busy to make a boat trip near it; now it would become my new office. Gnawing nervously on my first knuckle, I gave in for a second to the fear that I might not be up to this challenge. I swept my grandmother's picture off the desk and into my satchel, along with the latest book I was reading. My extensive research into mythology, combined with the burden of my parents' disappearance, left me unable to commit to one religion. Lifting my eyes to heaven in a brief prayer to Allah, on Kurnaz's behalf, since he was the believer, that he was fulfilling his duties, I stepped out into the hallway. Pushing aside these thoughts, I lifted my voice to summon my nursing staff. It was time to choose the five who would brave Kýz Kulesi with me.

The boat trip was less panic-inducing than the ride through the streets to the port in our hired supply wagon. After the first near miss, I could not bear to watch our progress through streets meant for pedestrians, so I spent more time watching the aeroflots chugging their way through the sky. The shrieks of my fellow nurses only seemed to encourage the maniac munching candied dates while snapping the reins. When we finally clambered out at the port, clutching at our supplies and bags, I made a point of giving the man the sharp side of my tongue. It did not improve my demeanor to discover that Kurnaz, being Kurnaz, had not waited. He'd taken the watchmen ahead to the island. I took a deep breath and tried to settle myself.

It soothed me some to have the well-spoken captain welcome me, and to watch his crew efficiently load our items aboard. As we pulled away from Haydarpaşa Port, I looked across the water to the Ayasofya mosque, its four great minarets, red-painted front, and gold-topped dome making it easily visible against the green hills. Then I turned to face my destination. Kýz Kulesi, the Maiden's Tower, awaited me. A part of me thrilled to be assigned to a site of such rich history. The rest of me feared I would be too stressed to appreciate it. In the distance, the Kongqi Long Chinese dirigible floated in slow circles above the Bosporus, a harsh reminder of my purpose here. A flash visible from the bow of the dirigible indicated it was responding to instructions from the port, most likely to wait until the docking rig was raised and anchored. Three smaller flashes came from the Ottoman airships. The rocking of the boats usually eased my cares, but today those were too many to calm.

Kurnaz waited at the dock to greet me as the boat pulled alongside the small rectangular island. I noticed that he'd found some cleaner clothes, and his moustaches were oiled enough that even the wind couldn't peel them from his cheeks. The wind did, however, whip his thinning hair. He flicked it out of his eyes as he reached forward to offer me a hand getting out of the boat. We both glanced up at the airships, whose drumming fans filled the air. To our left floated the barge loaded with the iron docking rig, and Kurnaz gestured toward it. "They will winch it upright and attach it to the wall so we can move things up and down, including their men. But first we must meet with them."

"This should be a peaceful setting, Kurnaz. The watchmen are here to do the work of setting up the tower, helping the nurses put together our field office, and provide for our safety if necessary. I want you to have them leave their guns behind. We mustn't provoke the Chinese. Things will be bad enough if they are carrying the plague."

"You know best, Mervat."

I tipped an eyebrow at him.

"When you are in charge, you know best."

"Fine, I would like to see the tower now," I said, turning away. This gave me a moment to consider the wall in front of me: the very wall from my second vision. It struck me that the first vision was likewise linked. The stairs I'd envisioned while in the Harbormaster's office could very well be those leading up the interior of the famed tower.

"Why the tower?" my cousin asked, anxious to get to the task at hand.

"So, I can see everything first before starting, and that is more easily done from above." That would hopefully be enough for him.

He gestured impatiently, and I followed him toward the lone building that occupied the island. Two stories tall, it was covered in white brick, with a few windows on the second floor. A red tiled roof covered the attached entrance area. On the left side rose the tower, four square stories, followed by a window-encircled cupola that was surrounded by a metal railing and surmounted by a flagpole. A navigational light stood opposite the tower on the corner of the island and a small pier accommodated incoming water traffic.

Rustling and bustling greeted me as I passed through the doors; my nurses already unpacking the supplies we'd brought with us. I frowned at the watchmen just standing along the walls inside while my nurses wrestled with the heavy crates. Kurnaz was looking from nurse to nurse, and I reached out to push him. "She's not here, you fool. Do you think that I would bring Salome along? You would get absolutely nothing done at all. I left her in charge at the hospital. In fact, speaking of getting nothing done, why are your men standing around like that? Get them to help the nurses or this will take forever." I rolled my eyes at him and scowled. "But first, get me the keys to the tower."

Shaking his head in amusement, Kurnaz began to loudly direct the guardsmen to and fro. One of them sheepishly approached me and offered the key before returning to the fray. I surveyed the activity for a moment, tables and cots being unfolded, supplies being unboxed and organized. Satisfied that things were happening as they should, I turned to the doorway in the far wall. With my suspicions raised by the vision, I had to be the first to see what mysteries the tower might hold.

The click of the key echoed, and the draft of warm air that rolled down the steps made me hesitate. I had expected it to be cold. Diffused light reached down from above but barely touched the darkness. I considered returning for a lamp, but the tower was only four stories tall. Surely, I could manage that.

On my first step, the stair creaked. My frown returned. If the steps were not safe, perhaps we should lock the tower to keep out the curious. As I climbed, the noise from the ground floor faded, then ceased. In fact, by the time I reached the turn that took me to the next floor, it was quiet enough that I heard the door snick shut below. Who was playing merry tricks now? With no light to see things below, I could only continue onward and hope there was a lantern to be found when I reached the rounded top floor. My outstretched hand caught the edge of a sill, and I pulled myself close to one of the archer-slit windows I'd seen from outside. It was so caked with dust that no light came through. Step by step, I proceeded upward. Halfway around, something brushed against the outside of my leg through my skirt. I stifled a scream with some difficulty. Hand over my mouth, I breathed heavily as yet another body wove about my ankles. Cats. A multitude of cats passed me, brushing against my legs. When I looked upward, all I could see was a sea of green, almond-shaped eyes staring at me out of the darkness—my vision manifested.

The little devils were everywhere. One stared at me out of the darkness from the sill I had just explored. I was determined that these felines were not going to stop me from reaching the top of the tower. I pushed myself forward. It was like wading through a warm and furry stream. The current of cats pushed against me in passing, but I hooked my arm under the railing to draw myself upward. One moment they were about my legs and the next they were up to my hips, then I was pulling myself hand over hand, gripping the railing, across their backs: my shoes no longer in contact with the stairs. Eyes zoomed at me out of the darkness, passing by in blurs. The muscles in my arms began to burn. The turn ahead indicated that I'd come all the way around the third floor. I still had two more flights of stairs ahead of me.

Amazed that none of the cats had scratched or nipped at me, I continued. I found myself stopping every few breaths to rest. The cats now slithered under my arms and across my back; fur brushing against my cheeks. Still, I pulled myself along, on and on. The first one that clambered across my head made me shriek, and at that moment, I began to wonder if it was possible to drown in cats. I hung there, so close to the final set of stairs, as if flung overboard and struggling to keep my head above waves of fur. When I felt the first of my fingers letting go, I realized that something had changed, the tide of cats receded. My feet once again touched the stairs. A little while longer and I could stand. Turning about, I considered the area below me, the entirety of the lower portion of the tower now writhed, a sea of fur punctuated by green-flashing eyes.

I caught my breath and pushed my protesting leg muscles onward; my hands numb from clutching so hard. *Fine, no way down. Well, my goal was upward, anyway.* I climbed until I could see the evening twilight filtering through the glass windows. Back hurting, snorting as if I had run the entire way, I popped my head above the level of the floor. I was surprised to find yet another set of green eyes staring at me.

A woman was stretched out upon a divan in the center of the round room. Her long black plaited hair fell in waves above a round golden necklace embossed with images of birds and beasts. She was such a surprise that I could only stare. The stranger's white chiton was cut in a style I only recognized from books. I tore my eyes away to glance around the room. Papyrus scrolls were stacked everywhere around the walls. Black pairs of gold-chased statuary cats stood guardian beside every entrance. A single brass telescope was propped in front of an open door. A bed of rushes lay against one wall. Pushing herself up to a seated position, the occupant of the room put her hands on the edge of the divan and stared at me. Only then did I realize that the woman's shadow cast by the setting sun did not match her profile but was in the shape of the head of a feline. I almost fell down the stairs. The clues were there from all of the mythology that I had studied, but how had a goddess of ancient Egypt come here to the Maiden's Tower? A light suddenly bloomed in my mind: why was she sending me visions?

The cat goddess's voice did not pass her lips. Instead, it rose from the stairwell below, a conglomeration of sounds from her hundreds of feline followers. The flow of fur on fur, claw on stone, gentle purrs, and all of the sounds that cats make. Together they blended. Slowly, recognizable words met my ears, "Well, aren't you determined."

"I am in need, oh Bast."

"There's a name that recent centuries have found little use for. You have my attention. Do approach. I can't have you skulking at the floor like a rodent."

Perhaps years of visions had made me more likely to believe in the impossible, I thought as I ascended. Once there, I leaned against the wall at the top of the stairs. *After all, I am conversing with a goddess. I haven't completely lost my mind, have I?* Before I could stop myself, I asked, "Why are you here of all places, Bast?"

"Come now, cats love heights, libraries, stories, and such. When I was chased out of Egypt all those years ago, I needed someplace new. Here was a lovely spot to retire to, after the burning of the library."

"Burning of — wait… Alexandria?"

"A truly fateful day. I called that magical place home until the flames came; a wonderful place to retire when my name stopped coming to the minds of the people. Like the many tomes of wisdom, my faith in men became ashes that day. Only after long consideration have I come to realize that not all are torch-bearing fools."

My eyes widened and my breath caught in my throat. The gods had left their lands when their people had stopped their worship. Were there other gods out there right now?

Bast purred loudly and her gaze caught mine. I found myself unable to look away. "You said that you have need?"

I needed the island, Bast's adopted home, but how could I ask that of this forgotten god? How could I ask Bast to share her haven? Finally, it all became clear. She was the source of the visions, and even if she had never set foot in Constantinople, she was still a divine influence that looked after people. Even if they were ignorant of her presence, they were a potential source of worship. She must have waited all these years until she divined that the time was right for her to intervene. A plan came to me. Since I was in the presence of a living goddess, it was difficult to say if it was truly my creation or divinely inspired. A goddess would help the people she perceived as hers; I could ask this. As I spoke, the green light of Bast's eyes began to glow.

When I came down from the tower, I found Kurnaz waiting for me. "Where have you been? Things have come to a boil. The Chinese sent a delegation. They used a cargo winch from their ship to drop down three men." With that, he caught my hand and drew me out past the examination areas my nurses had arranged. Kurnaz stood for a moment in the doorway. Ahead of him a group of guardsmen stood in a line, their black and red uniforms topped with red fezzes. Their rifles rested at their sides, butts on the ground. Damn Kurnaz. Hadn't I told him there were to be no guns?

Beyond them waited three Chinese in blue uniforms; the man in the middle's trimmed with gold brocade on the sleeves and shoulders. His hat was black with a red center, and a curved cavalry sword rested at his side. This wasn't a confrontation, but obviously neither side was comfortable with the current situation. "So far, they are not shooting," Kurnaz said, as he walked by my side past the watchmen's formation.

They would both put on a bold front, which was well enough. I'd dealt with plenty of men in dire straits. Injured parties who were so convinced they would never need anesthetic could be reasoned with and brought around. These were men who were frightened, and if they were good men, they had the best interests of their crew at heart. The fans of all the airships rumbled like distant thunder. To my left, I could see the barge bearing the docking tower. It would take quite a bit of engineering to get that upright, and that wasn't going to happen until I laid the groundwork. As Kurnaz and I approached, all three of the Chinese men were staring at me.

"Gentlemen," I said holding out my open hands.

"Where is the diplomat?" hissed the one on the right, "We've been forced to wait here and then they send us *you*? What is this? You act completely without honor. Do you fools not realize we have men starving to death above your very heads? The sick are without comfort and aid. This is intolerable. Do not press us into taking what we need. What happens will be upon your heads."

Kurnaz's eyes flew open wide, and his hand went immediately to his dagger. At the same time the man in the middle grasped the collar of the one who'd cried out, pulling him back, shoving him behind him. He looked at me, his eyes sharp and clear.

I stepped closer and said, "I am a nurse. I am sworn to aid the sick. My nurses and I are here to offer aid and to determine if you are carrying the plague. If you are not, then we can allow your ship into the port. If your men are sick, your ship will be quarantined. Your men can be treated here in a makeshift hospital we will set up in the building right over there. Regardless, we have both food and water coming on the boat you see behind us, so no one will starve."

I took a breath and then continued, "I am the administrator of my hospital, which means that I get things done. If you would rather wait for the diplomats who will spend their time talking and arguing, you are more than welcome. The harbormaster has sent me, so let's start accomplishing something."

For a moment nothing happened but the wind flapping through the sails, and then slowly, very slowly, the man in front of me smiled. He bowed and introduced himself, "I am Captain Shien Li of the Khongqi Long dirigible, the *Enduring Lotus Blossom*. It is always a pleasure to encounter someone who works with purpose. Please accept my apologies for my man. Like many of my crew, he is driven to extremes by the circumstances of our voyage. We will accept your terms. You may begin your examination with us, if that is suitable."

"I am pleased to meet someone who speaks our language so well, sir."

Li gestured about and said, "This is not my first trip to your city and hopefully it will not be my last."

I returned his bow and then turned to Kurnaz. "Please see that your watchmen stand aside. I will escort the captain and his men inside the building. Once they are ready, the nurses can begin the examination. Oh, and Kurnaz, I locked the tower. The stairs are not safe. Make sure the watchmen know that no one is to go up there."

Kurnaz nodded to me and then began shouting his instructions at the others. Well, I had chosen him, and I certainly should have known what I was in for.

"As for your ship, captain, I have a proposition to ensure that there are no rats aboard carrying the plague. I can send a great many cats aboard your vessel, and they will search out the vermin."

"That is a very clever solution to the problem."

"Well, sometimes one finds help in the most unexpected places."

"Indeed, madam. Indeed. My men will look forward to setting your furred warriors to their task." Li bowed low once again.

After returning his bow, I led the way to the examination area.

Several hours later, cages of burning rat corpses fell from the Khongqi Long dirigible into the waters of the Bosporus, and I understood my second vision. The feline representations of Bast had completed their task.

The *Enduring Lotus Blossom* was tethered to a tower at Haydarpaşa Port. Leaning against the railing of the top floor of the Maiden's Tower, I watched as the guardsmen pulled the temporary iron docking tower away from the wall. It would go back onto a barge for use elsewhere. Erhan had found my request somewhat unusual but hadn't balked. After all, I had produced results. Perhaps it was my influence that made the harbormaster agreeable or perhaps it was divine intervention. I had secured the Maiden's Tower for Bast. It seemed the least that I could do.

I felt the presence at my side of the tall Egyptian goddess. Bast regarded me kindly and then swept a feline glance in the direction of the gulls crying as they soared above the tower. From the corner of my eye, I caught the shadow of a tail flicking back and forth on the wall behind me.

"What will you do now?" I asked.

"What I always do, watch, doze, and occasionally read."

In a cat's eye, all things belong to cats, I thought. But there was still the question that would not leave. Why had she chosen me? Perhaps I was the key that made all that occurred possible, but there seemed to be something else. The revelation, when it came, was both humbling and surprising: I was the only one who would have immediately recognized her and trusted her. Since I was a witness to her actions and abilities, I could tell the story of how she had helped to avert the crisis. I could plant the seed to revive the worship of the goddess of cats. Did I, the hospital administrator, wish to become a prophet for a once-forgotten god? I had a suspicion that there might be further visions forthcoming. Then something occurred to me: Bast was a goddess tied to her nature. If I wished to avoid such a future, then I must distract her. "You've been here observing us for so long. You could always cross the water and see the city."

"Why would I do that?"

"Well, it came to me that if you represent yourself as a cat and most people see you in such a fashion, that perhaps one of your family could have already found a new home here in Constantinople."

Bast drew back from me, but I noted a curious longing in her eyes.

"There are a great many dogs running about the city. Could it be that your brother, Anubis, is here?" I had her now, but how long could I distract a goddess? Well, we would just have to see.

Bast pursed her lips and once again the shadow tail flickered. "Isn't that a thing, a thing indeed?" Her green eyes were sharp with intent. "I don't suppose there is room on your boat?"

"Oh, certainly," I said, "We'll just make Kurnaz stay until the next trip."

Bonnie and Clyde

ABOUT THE AUTHORS

Marc L Abbott is a Brooklyn native horror author. He is the co-author of *Hell at Brooklyn Tea* and the two-time African American Literary Award-winning horror anthology, *Hell at the Way Station*. His horror short stories are featured in the anthologies *Blackened Roots, A Woman Unbecoming, Soul Scream, Even in the Grave,* and the Bram Stoker Nominated horror anthologies *New York State of Fright & Under Twin Suns: Alternate Histories of the Yellow Sign*. His new horror novel, *Sinister Ascension* from Mocha Memoirs Press, is out now. He is a 2015 Moth Story Slam and Grand Slam Storyteller winner and an award-winning actor. When he is not curating workshops for the Center for Fiction, he teaches writing to students at Dr. Izquierdo Health and Science Charter School. Find out more about him at www.whoismarclabbott.com

Award-winning author, editor, and publisher **Danielle Ackley-McPhail** has worked both sides of the publishing industry for longer than she cares to admit. In 2014 she joined forces with Mike McPhail and Greg Schauer to form eSpec Books (www.especbooks.com).

Her published works include eight novels, ten solo collections, three writers' guides, and two cookbooks. She is a former member of the Science Fiction and Fantasy Writers Association and a current member of the Horror Writers Association.

Danielle lives in New Jersey with husband and fellow writer, Mike McPhail and four extremely spoiled rescue cats.

Rigel Ailur writes in almost every genre, but mostly science fiction and fantasy. Her short story credits include "Brigadoon" in the *Star Trek* anthology *Strange New Worlds 10,* "Building Bridges" in the IAMTW's *Turning the Tied,* and "Class Project" in *Double Trouble: An Anthology of*

Two-Fisted Team-Ups. The Angel Cat Collection includes two stories by her, and the *Lady Pirates* omnibus *Pirates!* includes four of her stories, two about the Queen of the pirates in the Asian seas, and two about Medieval English river pirates. Her novel *Azure Dragon* takes place in contemporary America, and the many novels and short stories of her *Tales of Mimion* series, including one auf Deutsch, take place on that planet. Above all, she treasures her most beloved swarm of cats. Visit http: BluetrixBooks.com for more information and a complete bibliography.

Grace Bridges is a fantasy and sci-fi author, a professional fiction editor, and is currently responsible for five cats. She lives in New Zealand's magical geothermal heart amongst geysers and hot springs, and often sets her stories there. Previously she has fostered cats and kittens for Gutter Kitties, an Auckland-based rescue group. A three-time winner of the Sir Julius Vogel Award from the Science Fiction and Fantasy Association of New Zealand, she also belongs to the Rotorua Arts Village Collective and is a life member of writers' association Speculative Fiction New Zealand (SpecFicNZ) after serving as its president for seven years. www.gracebridges.kiwi.

Christopher J. Burke is a math teacher, a webcomic creator, and writer from Brooklyn, where he does a lot of walking. He cowrote GURPS *Autoduel* for Steve Jackson Games, and his work has appeared in in *Daily Science Fiction, MetaStellar, Science Fiction Lampoon, Free Flash Fiction, MAD Magazine,* and the anthology *Devilish & Divine* (eSpec Books). His books include *In A Flash 2020* and *A Bucket Full of Moonlight* from eSpec Books. He's self-published five short fantasy books in a series called Burke's Lore Briefs, the latest of which is *Yesterday's Villains.*

Artist **Amber Davis** currently fosters for the South Jersey Regional Animal Shelter, in Vineland, NJ.

Keith R.A. DeCandido has, in his time, provided food and shelter for ten cats, one dog, and one fish, including the two current kitties, Kaylee and Louie, both incredibly sweet black cats. When he's not feeding, cuddling, or scritching the pair of them, he writes, edits, performs music, and practices martial arts. His recent and upcoming fiction includes the new urban fantasy series *Supernatural Crimes Unit: NYPD,* which debuted in the fall of 2025; *Phoenix Precinct* and *Feat of Clay,* the latest in two other fantasy series of his, also published by eSpec; the *Resident Evil* graphic novel *Infinite Darkness: The Beginning;* the short-story collection *Ragnarok and a Hard Place: More Tales of Cassie Zukav, Weirdness Magnet*; a new novel series about superheroes in 1970s New York, *The Inflictors*; multiple short stories in the magazines *Weird Tales* and *Star Trek Explorer* and in the anthology series *Sherlock Holmes: Cases by Candlelight*, *Sherlock Holmes: Eliminate the Impossible*, *Thrilling Adventure Yarns*, *Defending the Future*, *Phenomenons*, and *Forgotten Lore*; and stories in the standalone anthologies *The Green Hornet & Kato: Detroit Noir City*, *Multiverse of Mystery*, *Farscape 25th Anniversary Special*, *Jukebox Thrillers: Solid Hits of the 80s!*, *PRISM: The Mission Files*, and *Weird Tales: 100 Years of Weird*. Keith also writes about pop culture for the award-winning web site Reactor Magazine (formerly Tor.com), for his Patreon (patreon.com/krad), and for various essay collections published by Becky Books, Crazy 8 Press, ATB Publishing, and Sequart. In addition, Keith is a martial artist (a fourth-degree black belt in karate), a musician (currently percussionist with the parody band Boogie Knights and the rock band The Chris Abbott Band), and an editor of more than thirty years' standing (though he usually does it sitting down). Find out less at DeCandido.net.

Carol Gyzander is a Bram Stoker Award® winning horror author/anthologist of twisted tales that touch your heart. Her stabby feminist anthology, *Discontinue If Death Ensues*, is a World Fantasy Award finalist, and her "Bobblehead" poem is a Rhysling Award finalist. As HWA-NY Chapter Co-Chair, she co-hosts their Galactic Terrors reading series.

Lisa Kruse has a masters degree in accounting and worked for a firm doing payroll & business taxes until she was diagnosed with an aggressive form of multiple sclerosis in 2010. She is now in a wheelchair full-time and can no longer drive (along with many other issues unfortunately). She spends her time taking care of the inside cats and trying to fight this terrible disease.

For nearly 50 years, until his death in 2024, **Sharon Lee** and Steve Miller lived, wrote, and kept cats together. Working on the theory that you can't have enough of a good thing, they brought cats in to comfort and confound the large cast of characters inhabiting the Liaden Universe®, their long-running space opera. Likewise, Sharon made sure cats were represented in her single-authored fantasy trilogy and cozy mystery duology. "Ginger and the Bully of Lowergate Court," which appears in this volume, is unique in Lee and Miller cat tales because it actually happened. Yes, exactly the way I said.

Mike McPhail's love of the science fiction genre sparked a life-long interest in science, technology, and developing an understanding of the human condition—all of which played an important role in his writing, art, and game design. He is best known as the creator and series editor of the award-winning Defending the Future military science fiction anthologies—now in their second decade of publication. His body of work has been formally recognized with his acceptance into SFWA, the Science Fiction and Fantasy Writers of America.

Much to his embarrassment, **Bernie Mojzes** has outlived Lord Byron, Percy Shelley, Janice Joplin, and the Red Baron, without even once having been shot down over Morlancourt Ridge. Having failed to achieve a glorious martyrdom, he has instead turned his hand to the penning of prose, an example of which you currently hold in your hands. Or is perhaps being projected from an electronic device perched atop your stationary bicycle or treadmill as a distraction from such mundane, repetitive tasks. Since undertaking this labor, he has had a small bushel of short stories published in anthologies and various online venues (37 when he stopped counting in 2014), and has himself published the now-defunct online zine, *Unlikely Story*, and edited two anthologies: *Clowns: The Unlikely Coulrophobia Remix*, and *The Flesh Made Word*. His first full-length endeavor, *Mistress of Bees*, was released in 2025 (and he does very much hope you'll read it (even though he hasn't managed to put it on his long out-of-date website, www.kappamaki.com (which he has been failing to update for many years—maybe someday that will change.)))

Nancy Jane Moore is the author of the fantasy novel *For the Good of the Realm*, the science fiction novel *The Weave*, and the novella *Changeling*, all from Aqueduct Press. Her short fiction has appeared in a number of anthologies and magazines and in her collection from PS Publishing, *Conscientious Inconsistencies*. A native Anglo Texan, she lived in Washington, DC, for many years and now lives with her sweetheart in Oakland, California. She has lived with a variety of cats, many of whom just showed up one day. Currently she is working on a sequel to *For the Good of the Realm*.

Aaron Rosenberg is the best-selling, award-winning author of over 50 novels, including the Twin Cities Cryptids urban fantasy/cozy series, the DuckBob SF comedy series, the Relicant Chronicles epic fantasy series, the Areyat Islands fantasy pirate mystery series, the upcoming BEO Files urban fantasy series, and, with David Niall Wilson, the *O.C.L.T.* occult thriller series. His tie-in work contains novels for *Star Trek*, *Warhammer*, *World of WarCraft*, *Stargate: Atlantis*, *Shadowrun*, *Mutants & Masterminds*, and *Eureka* and short stories for *The X-Files*, *World of Darkness*, *Crusader Kings II*, *Deadlands*, *Master of Orion*, and *Europa Universalis IV*. He has written children's books (including the original series STEM Squad and Pete and Penny's Pizza Puzzles, the award-winning *Bandslam: The Junior Novel* and the #1 best-selling *42: The Jackie Robinson Story*), educational books, and roleplaying games (including the original games *Asylum*, *Spookshow*, and *Chosen*; work for White Wolf, Wizards of the Coast, Fantasy Flight, Pinnacle, and many others; the Origins Award-winning *Gamemastering Secrets*; and the Gold ENnie-winning *Lure of the Lich Lord*). He is a founding member of Crazy 8 Press. Aaron lives in New York with his family. You can follow him online at gryphonrose.com, on Facebook at facebook.com/gryphonrose, on BSky at @gryphonrose.bsky.social, on Instagram at the_gryphon-rose, and on X (formerly known as Twitter) @gryphonrose.

Lawrence M. Schoen holds a Ph.D. in cognitive psychology, is a past Astounding, Hugo, and Nebula finalist, twice won the Cóyotl award for best novel, founded the Klingon Language Institute, and occasionally does work as a hypnotherapist specializing in authors' issues.

His science fiction includes many light and humorous adventures of a space-faring stage hypnotist and his alien animal companion. Other works take a very different tone, exploring aspects of determinism and free will, generally redefining the continua between life and death. Sometimes he blurs the funny and the serious. He believes "Cat Futures" may be as near a perfect story as he's ever written.

Lawrence and his wife live just outside Philadelphia, Pennsylvania. Recently he has bested both Multiple Myeloma and Leukemia. He is a chimeric cancer survivor. The Universe isn't done with him.

Jean Marie Ward writes fiction, nonfiction and everything in be-tween, including novels, art books, and military strategy. (That one surprised her too.) The former editor of Crescent Blues and currently author interviewer for BookBale.com, she co-edited the six-volume, 40th anniversary World Fantasy Con anthology *Unconventional Fantasy*. If you like what you've read here, two more X-Cat stories can be found in her short story collection, *Dragons, Cats, and Formidable Femmes*. Learn more at JeanMarieWard.com.

Jeff Young is a bookseller first and a writer second – although he wouldn't mind a reversal of fortune.

He is an award-winning author who has contributed to the anthologies: *Afterpunk, In an Iron Cage: The Magic of Steampunk, Clockwork Chaos, Gaslight and Grimm, Phantasmical Contraptions and other Errors, By Any Means, Best Laid Plans, Dogs of War, Man and Machine, If We Had Known, Fantastic Futures 13, The Society for the Preservation of C.J. Henderson, Eccentric Orbits 2 & 3, Writers of the Future V.26, TV Gods and TV Gods: Summer Programming.* Jeff's own fiction is collected in *Spirit Seeker, Written in Light* and TOI *Special Edition 2 – Diversiforms.* He has also edited the *Drunken Comic Book Monkey* line, *TV Gods* and *TV Gods –Summer Programming* and is the managing editor for the magazine, *Mendie the Post-Apocalyptic Flower Scout.* He has led the Watch the Skies SF&F Discussion Group of Camp Hill and Harrisburg for twenty-five years.

Magnus and Curio

OUR COOL CATS COLONY

Alexander Hale
Alp Beck
Amanda Sedivy
Amelia B.
Andreja and Duke
Andrew Hatchell
Andrew Kaplan
Anna Marie Stern
April Sue Billings
Aunty Meow
Beth Lobdell
Bethany Jezerey
Brad Ackerman
Brendan Lonehawk
Brooks Moses
Bunrab
Caroline Westra
Carrilyn Thorpe
Catherine Asaro
Cathy Green
Cheryl Lynn Chessie Jones
Christopher J. Burke
Colleen Feeney
Connor Lehmann
Craig Hackl
Danielle Ackley-McPhail
David Lee Summers and Kumie Wise
DC
Deborah A. Flores
Dev Singer
Dianne Nicholson

Dr. Karen
Ed Ellis
Ef Deal
Elyse M Grasso
Florentina
George Minor (Aspen & Daisy)
GhostCat
Gillian Daniels
Gina DeSimone
Giusy Rippa
Glori Medina
Harriet McDermott
Holly
Ivy Ru
Ixias
Jacob Jones-Goldstein
Janice and T Campbell
Jeffrey Harlan
Jeremy Audet
Jeremy Bottroff
Jerrie the filkferengi
Joanne B Burrows
Jonathan H. Bruck
Joshua McGinnis
Juanita J Nesbitt
Judy A Lauer
Judy McClain
Katy Manck
Kay Hafner
Kris smelser
Leanna Renee Hieber
Lee Hawkridge

Linda Pierce
Lisa Kruse
Lorraine J. Anderson
Louise & Ruby McCulloch
Lynn P
maileguy
Margaret Bumby
Margot Harris
Marie Devey
Mark Woodson
Mary Anne Howard
mdtommyd
Melynda Marchi
Michael Gordon
Michael S. Rosenberg
Mike McPhail,
    McP Digital Graphics
Nellie Batz
Norman Jaffe
Paksenarrion
Peter Piine Graham
pjk
Reckless Pantalones
Richard Novak
Robert H Hudson Jr

Ronald H. Miller
Ruth Ann Orlansky
Sabrina White
Samantha J Bryant
Sarolta
Shawnee M
Sheryl R. Hayes
SilverWolf28
Sonya Lawson
Stacey Helton
Stephanie Wood Franklin
Stephen W. Chappell
Steven Purcell
Taj S.
Tanya Koenig
The Initiative Inn
The Watanabe Clowder
Tina M Noe Good
Tory Shade
Tracy Popey
Tracy 'Rayhne' Fretwell
Trip Space-Parasite
W. Scott Meeks
Walter J. Montie
Zilla

Baby

HOW CAN YOU HELP?
GLAD YOU ASKED!

Not up to cat rescue field work?
There are still plenty of ways you can help.

Volunteer at your local shelter.

Foster, if you are able.

Donate rags or blankets.

Look up your local shelter or rescue's online Wish List and
donate something they need.

If you see an animal in distress, call your local rescue, or at
least the police non-emergency line.

Pick up volume two, *More Futures for Ferals*, to learn more
about cat rescue and also help us help them!

Tell people about these charity anthologies
so we can do more to help the cause.

All profits from *A Future for Ferals* and *More Futures for Ferals*
will be donated to cat rescue organizations and shelters.

(Cuddle) Bug is very happy to see you made it this far.